SAVAGE HEART

BORN VILLAINS
BOOK ONE

ABBI COOK

SAVAGE HEART

He told me our time together wasn't over.

Alaric Rule is a killer, a hitman for the crime syndicate his uncle controls. He offers no mercy for anyone in his sights.

But to me, he's the man who gave me a chance to have the life I want.

I'm valuable to the Rossetti family because I can be traded, given away by my brother to a man who can benefit him.

A prize valued merely for my body.

Now only a man like Alaric Rule can help me. I pray our time together isn't over yet.

CHAPTER ONE

ienna

THE LAST HOURS OF MY LIFE IN COLLEGE ARE ticking away, and I feel like there's not enough time to get everything done. In two years, I've succeeded in becoming the person I always knew I could be, but now school is coming to an end, and all I can think is I wanted to do so much more.

Here, I'm Sabrina Marshall, art history major with a minor in French and a position lined up as a translator for a Fortune 500 company after graduation. I'm successful, at the top of my class, and the girl who always has a smile for everyone.

Not Sienna Rossetti, daughter of a father who hated her so much he put a hit out on her. Sister of four stepbrothers who never cared for me either.

1

Stepdaughter to a kept woman who never liked me because I'm the evidence of my father's interest in a better woman.

I've thought a lot about my mother in the past two years here at Yale. Every so often, I search her name online to see how she's doing. Being the wife of a president suits her, if the pictures I've seen are any indication. She's as beautiful as ever with her long, dark hair without a hint of gray to be found and those stunning deep brown eyes made even more gorgeous by makeup. I wish I could tell her I'm alive and doing well here, but I can't risk it.

For now, I have to remain what I hope is a loving memory that makes her smile when she thinks of me.

I searched for my father too. The one and only time I did, my stomach twisted into a tight knot that threatened to make me vomit as the thought of him wanting me dead filled me again. I pushed that terrible memory aside and scrolled through the news reports from home that detailed how he was killed only a week after he betrayed me. I know who did that.

Alaric.

Every night for the first few months here, I waited for him to appear at my door. He must know where I live. It's his family who pays for this apartment and my school. Then for the next few months, I told myself it's better that he doesn't come here. He's a part of my life I should forget.

But I've never been able to forget Alaric.

After a while, I convinced myself that Helix never

told him where I live or who I am now. That would explain why in two years Alaric has never come to see me.

Sometimes I think I've sensed him nearby watching out for me to make sure I'm safe. That's probably not true, though. Why would he? We only spent a couple days together. He's likely forgotten them and me.

If only I could say the same.

His family checks on me from time to time, like some distant relation they aren't sure how to approach but feel some responsibility toward even they don't understand. His uncle Nick drops by to tell me if I need anything he's the one to call, but I require nothing that money can buy. Helix took care of that. My school is paid for, along with this apartment, and that day he left me at the airport in Hartford, he handed me a wad of cash and a checkbook for an account that always has more than enough money in it.

What I need doesn't seem to need or want me anymore.

I shake my head to dispel that thought from my mind or I'll start crying, and that's not what I want to do tonight. This night is for celebration with my friends I've made here at school.

I've had to lie to nearly every person I've met since coming here, not to hurt them but to keep me safe. With my father's death right after I left Italy, my brother Matteo took charge of our family. Of the family business. He's never tried to contact me, but I know deep in my bones that the day is coming when he'll appear to take me back to the family.

Even though that's the last thing I want.

"Hey, girl! Did you hear what I said?"

I turn to look at Natasha in my doorway and shake my head as she stares at me with beautiful blue eyes that never fail to look completely sincere. "I'm sorry. I got lost in my head there for a minute. What's up?"

She smiles and rolls her eyes. "You've been doing that a lot lately. Feeling sentimental about leaving good old Yale? I don't know why you would be. You've got a great job lined up, unlike me with my million and a half resumes out in the wilderness doing nothing but growing dust on people's desks."

I smile and can't help but tease her. "Does anyone actually print resumes out anymore? I thought we'd left that behind in the last century."

Natasha has always seemed like an old soul, and her choice of pursuing journalism as a major fits right in with her feeling like she's from another time and place. Not that people don't write pieces for newspapers and magazines, but I thought they had all gone online years ago. She loves to correct me with exactly what comes out of her mouth right now.

"Physical resumes, like print, are not dead, contrary to the reports of their demise."

Only she could sound cute and say things our seventy-five-year-old American Literature professor might say.

"Well, I doubt they're getting dusty anywhere. Before you know it, you're going to be at the New York Times, and where will I be? Interpreter for a Fortune 500 company and wondering if I should have majored in something other than art history," I say, not afraid to show her how utterly terrified I am that I wasted the past two years of my life at one of the best universities in the world pursuing a passion instead of a subject that leads to a nice paycheck.

She waves away my concerns. "You worry too much. You're fluent in three languages, Sabrina. Three! I only know one, so where's that leave me? And you already have a job waiting for you right after graduation. I wish I could say that."

Sabrina. It's been two years since Helix Rule handed me all the papers that say I'm Sabrina Marshall, and still to this day I have to remind myself not to look around when someone says that name. I swear if someone yelled Sienna right now, I'd spin my head like some kind of possessed doll.

It happened once in class last semester. Someone called out for some girl named Sienna at the back of the classroom, and I spun around like he was talking to me.

Old habits die hard, especially when they're the simplest and purest meaning of who you are.

"Are you coming to meet up with Ash and a few of her bio friends? She swears they're hysterical when they aren't under pressure and always studying, so I think we should put that theory to the test."

As much as it could be fun to sit with Natasha and quietly make jokes about how completely stressed out those science people are, even now that nearly all finals are over, I force a smile and shake my head. "I'm going to have to take a rain check on that. I have too much to get finished around here."

Natasha shrugs and turns to leave. "You probably won't miss too much. Those bio people are boring, but I swear ever since Ash started going out with Noah, she can't seem to see that anymore."

Looking back at me, she smiles and adds, "I have a feeling Jesse might be there with them. Does that make you change your mind at all?"

I shake my head and smile at her attempt to get me to admit I still have any interest in Jesse McCallister. Tall, dark, and full of himself, I ended up at a party with him in an attempt to forget about Alaric right after I arrived here at Yale. Big mistake. Jesse has a one-track mind, and after our single time together, I wanted off that train. He didn't, though, and ever since, he's been around as much as he can arrange in the hope that I'll change my mind and want to try another round of mediocre sex with him.

Sorry, Jesse. I had someone rock my world once, and you don't come close, sadly.

"Did you forget about Trent? We've been dating for almost six months."

Natasha cringes and shakes her head. "I'm sorry. I don't know why I never think of him. It's probably because you never bring him around to hang out."

Her excuse is a valid one. I've been seeing Trent Michaels since last semester, but we've never hung out with my friends in all that time. He's not the partying type. In fact, he's not really the type to want to do much at all. Trent's more of a workaholic. I don't even know if he'll be able to get away from the office to attend graduation. I gave him a ticket, but the best he could promise was, "We'll see."

"Okay, I'll be back later and maybe we can do something then. Toodles!"

Again with the talking like she's from another time. It's all part of her charm, though. I just hope Jesse doesn't try his routine on her today. Natasha deserves so much better.

She deserves an Alaric.

I PLUCK MY EARBUDS OUT AND STUFF THEM INTO the pocket of my hoodie as I spin around to see if someone's behind me. I'm alone in my apartment, but I could have sworn I felt a person behind me.

All this emotion about leaving school is making me squirrely. I wasn't playing my music that loud that I wouldn't have heard someone walk in.

Relax, Sienna. I mean Sabrina.

Jesus, you'd think after almost two years that I'd have that routine down cold.

I glance over at my desk beneath the window. How many hours did I spend sitting there hidden behind those while cellular shades as I studied? The bent section on the lefthand side is evidence of how many times I peered out hoping for once to see him standing out on the grass for me.

He told me our time together wasn't over, but he's never appeared again. No matter how many times I've checked, he's never there.

All week, I've wondered if maybe he'd show up. Does he even know I'm graduating in a couple days? Then again, with how he feels about Ivy League people, he likely wouldn't care even if he did know.

I'm foolish to hope for something that's never going to happen. Two years have passed since that night we stood in that hotel lobby and I told him I loved him. I don't regret that, but it's clear the reason he didn't say he loved me back is our time together didn't mean as much to him as it did me.

He moved on and as much as it appears I have too, I haven't. It's time I do, though.

A knock at my front door tears me out of my thoughts, thankfully. Helix made sure to get me an apartment in a secure building, so I don't have to worry about who's waiting for me in the hallway. It's probably Trent. He did say he'd stop over tonight if he got finished with work early enough.

I open the door as I say, "I'm glad you tore yourself away from your desk." But it isn't Trent standing in front of me.

It's the man I've waited two years to see.

CHAPTER TWO

ienna

THE SIGHT OF HIM TAKES MY BREATH AWAY, AND I step back from the door in shock. After all those times I waited for him, finally Alaric has found me once again.

He looks the same as he did the last time I saw him. His dark eyes stare into mine, and I shake my head, unable to believe this is happening. Two years and he suddenly shows up at my door just days before I graduate.

"Sienna."

No one's called me that name in so long that just hearing it makes me want to burst into tears. Pushing away the need to cry, I shake my head again. "It's

Sabrina now. I guess your uncle liked that name, so he gave it to me. Sabrina Marshall."

Without me asking him to come in, he steps across the threshold and gently closes the door behind him, as if this is as much his home as it is mine. It's like he takes up all the oxygen in the room simply by being him. Like I can't get enough air into my lungs now that he's in here with me.

"Why are you here now?" I choke out as he takes a step toward me and then another.

I want to add after all this time, but I don't. I can't say those words for some reason.

Alaric takes another step toward me and stops. With a smile, he answers, "I have something for you. For your graduation, I mean."

"You know I'm graduating? Have you known I've been here in this apartment the whole time?"

My emotions spin inside me, whirling from sad to angry when he nods his answer to my question. "You knew the whole two years and never once came to see me? And now you show up with what? A graduation card and a twenty-dollar bill? Thanks. Feel free to leave it on the table on your way out."

I want him to say something so I can lash out, but he stays silent, simply staring at me. We stand there like that for what seems like forever until he slides his hand into his coat pocket and pulls out a tiny black box.

"Seemed only right to replace the one I took from

you, and what better time to do it than now?" he says in a low voice.

When he hands the box to me, I don't know what to say. I want to be angry with him, but he just gave me a gift.

"Open it. I think you'll like it."

I slowly lift the lid off the box and see a gold cross on a necklace nestled in white silk inside. He bought me a gold cross because he took mine that day.

As tears fill my eyes, I look up at him and ask, "Do you still have my old one?"

He nods and stuffs his hand into his pocket. A second later, he pulls out the gold cross that fell off in the shower at his villa in Italy. The necklace is nowhere to be found, but the cross is shinier than ever.

"You kept my gold cross all this time? Why?"

Alaric shrugs. "Because it was all I had of you. I carry it everywhere with me."

Tears stream out of my eyes at his confession that he hasn't forgotten me either, and I cover my face with my hands to hide how much hearing those words means to me. "I was sure you never even thought of me these past two years."

"I told you I wouldn't forget you, Sienna."

The sound of my true name coming out of his mouth makes me smile, like a memory from long ago that never fails to bring happiness. "It's been so long since anyone called me that."

Walking over to me, he sighs as his hands cradle my face. "I'm sorry I didn't come before now."

I look up into his dark eyes and a million questions race through my mind. "Why didn't you? If you were thinking of me, did you think I wasn't doing the same about you?"

He doesn't answer for a long moment, but finally he says, "I didn't think someone like me had any place in your world."

"And I didn't have any place in yours?"

Alaric nods, swallowing hard so his Adam's apple drops and then rises again. "I am what I am, Sienna. You deserved a chance to have a fresh start here. But I made sure to keep tabs on you. I've never been very far away, and if you ever needed me, I would have come before now."

I lower my head as tears fill my eyes again. "I did need you. Not to protect me but because I missed you."

"Well, you seem to have done fine. You're only a couple days away from graduation, and you moved on, so I assumed you didn't need me."

His words come out ragged and choppy, and when I look up at him, I see his jaw clenched. Is he actually upset I moved on after all that time?

Anger surges through me, so I push my hands against his chest and step back away. "I needed you, Alaric! Was I supposed to just sit around in this Yale location of Chez Helix and simply wait for you? You knew where I was this whole time and never came to me. I didn't know where you were, because if I did, I damn sure would have taken the opportunity to see you."

My outburst leaves him confused, and he simply stands there shaking his head. "I don't want to fight you on this, Sienna. I had to do what I did. I won't apologize for that."

"And I won't apologize for wanting to be cared about. If you didn't want me to meet someone, you should have come around. You didn't, so I have a man in my life now."

God, this isn't how I wanted our reunion to go. I played out this scene in my head so many times I wondered on occasion if it had actually occurred it felt so real, but now that it's actually happening, it's more anger than love.

Through gritted teeth, Alaric mutters, "Trent. Sounds like a Yale asshole if I've ever of heard one."

"You don't even know him, so what gives you the right to say anything about him? He's never been cruel or unkind to me, and he makes me happy."

Alaric steps forward, pressing his body to mine, and looks down into my eyes. "Happy? Does he make you forget the world exists when the two of you are together? Because that's what we had, Sienna."

I wince as my body betrays me, filling with desire for him. My breath gets caught in my chest, so I answer with a shake of my head.

There's no point in lying. Trent has never made me feel like Alaric did. At first, I couldn't help but miss that, but in time, I grew to accept that no one was ever going to affect me like Alaric did back in Italy.

But that was a different time and a different place. Now I have someone gentle and kind who cares for me.

"A man doesn't have to take my breath away to make me happy. If you had bothered to come see me in the past two years, you'd know that."

He lifts his hand toward my chin and drags his fingertip along my jaw, making my eyelids flutter closed at his tender touch. "You deserve nothing less than a man who takes your breath away. Why are you so willing to settle for common and mediocre when you've had incredible and unforgettable? *We* had incredible and unforgettable, Sienna."

I sigh heavily, hating how right he is. "Because that never showed up and I got lonely, Alaric."

"You don't care about him. I can tell."

"What makes you think you can say that?" I ask angrily.

His hand slides around my neck before he closes his fingers around my hair, sending waves of pain and need skittering across my scalp. "I can say that because I know you, Sienna. You're mine, and no time you spend with some bland guy can change that."

"Yours?"

Good to know that being his means he ignores me for years.

"Mine."

The look on his face tells me he actually means

that. I'm not willing to let myself be assumed to be his, though, so I step back from him, instantly missing his touch.

"Just admit the truth. You didn't care enough about me after I flew away from Italy to come find me. I'm guessing it's because I told you I loved you. Typical man. Feel free to forget I ever said that."

Still, he won't let this go.

Shaking his head, he cages my body in against the wall with his body and smiles down at me. "How do you know I didn't fall in love with you in the time we spent together? Just because I didn't say it back?"

Sincerity fills his dark eyes, and I so want to believe he cared about me like I cared about him. But I can't let myself fall for that.

"Uh, yeah. That's how people know if the feeling is returned. I might not have a line of men a mile long I've had great sex with, but I do know that."

My words get stuck in my throat as I speak, mostly from jealousy since I'm sure he's been with dozens of women since our time in Italy. I shouldn't care. So we spent a couple days together and he saved my life? It probably happens a lot in his world.

"Don't think for a second I didn't fall for you. I didn't say it back because the life I lead doesn't allow for that kind of thing."

God, he sounds so earnest when he says that!

"Then why are you here tonight?" I ask, loving the feel of his body pressing against mine.

His dark eyes fill with need. "I couldn't let your big

day go by without bringing you a gift. I missed you, Sienna. Never doubt that."

I want to believe that. He has no idea how much it means to me to hear him say those words. But it doesn't change the fact that for two years I've waited for him to return.

Quietly, I ask, "Why couldn't you just let me keep thinking I meant nothing to you? At least then I could hate you."

Not that I ever truly felt anything close to that.

CHAPTER THREE

laric

"I'VE WAITED ALL THIS TIME TO SEE YOU AGAIN," I say in her ear. "I'm sorry I waited so long."

Her anger melts away as tears fill her beautiful eyes I've missed looking at me. "I love my gift. Thank you. And I love that you kept my old cross all this time."

"I never forgot you or how you made me feel for those few days. I just thought you'd be better off without me since you were here at Yale and living your dream."

Sienna shakes her head. "I wish you didn't stay away. I may not be right for your world, but you would have been great here for me because I have no one other than a few friends."

"And your boyfriend," I say, each word drenched in jealousy.

She hears it come through loud and clear and sighs. "You leave me alone for two years, and you think you should be upset about me having a boyfriend? Do they make sure hitmen have balls the size of Texas before they let you do the job, or are you just naturally like this?"

I wrap my hand around her neck and gently squeeze my fingers into her soft skin. "Possessive? I'm just naturally that way."

Her eyes flutter closed, and she winces, but it's not from pain. She's missed my touch as much as I've missed hers, and that boyfriend be damned.

"You have no idea how much I wished you would come to me and say that during all those months alone, Alaric," she whispers softly.

"I never left you, Sienna. Not really."

Lifting her hand to my chest, I press her palm over my heart. "You were always right here with me."

When she opens her eyes, I see they're glassy from tears. I never dreamed she'd miss me as much as I missed her. She had an entire life to create here at Yale, so I assumed she'd find new friends and make her way. The idea of her finding someone else was never something I spent much time on, but not because I didn't think she would.

I knew she'd move on. She had every right to, and even to these Ivy League assholes, she stands out because of her beauty and brains. I knew one of them would convince her to forget about me.

So I pushed that out of my head and went on with my life. But now that I'm here with her and she's so close, I can't ignore how much I hate the mere thought of some guy touching her.

"Tell me the truth, Alaric. My father's death. Was that you who did it?" she asks, and I sense a hint of sadness under her words.

I nod, honest with her as I've been from nearly the moment I met her. "It was me."

"Why?"

My two hands slide up her neck to cradle her face. "Because he tried to hurt someone I care about. That's why."

"You knew me for less than three days, Alaric."

I shrug and answer with the only thing I know to be true about how I feel. "Feelings aren't ruled by time."

"I understand that. I fell in love with you in that short time we spent together. You did more to care for me in just a few hours than my family had done my entire life."

"And I'd do it all again in a heartbeat."

That makes her smile. "I've missed the way you can be so certain about everything. I never feel that way. Every part of my life is full of second guesses and wondering if I should have done things differently."

With a smile, I nod again. She has no idea what I'd do to keep her safe and how much I've cared about her all this time. "I'm certain about you, Sienna. And I'm certain that I won't let anyone hurt you."

Worry makes her frown as she says, "You must know that my brother Matteo has taken over the family. I'm scared all the time that he's going to send one of his goons after me."

"You don't have to worry about that. My family and I have watched over you to make sure he can't get to you."

A curious look fills her eyes as she stares up at me now. "So you've known about Trent the whole time I've been with him?"

That name makes rage course through me, so I step back away from her as my hands instinctively ball into tight fists. "Yeah, and to be honest, on top of him being out of his league with you, he seems suspect to me."

"Suspect? Why?"

As much as I want to say I checked him out and found he's in league with her family back in Italy, that's not true. The fucker seems utterly clean. No police record. No hint of ties to Matteo and the rest of the Rossettis. Fuck, on paper, he's the perfect guy for Sienna.

So, naturally, I hate him.

"Let's just say I'm suspicious," I answer, avoiding her gaze as I pretend to look out the window.

"Suspicious because he's a bad man, or suspicious because you just don't like him?" she asks with a smile in her voice.

I turn around to see her grinning at me. Jesus, she's even more beautiful when she smiles.

"Let's just say I don't like him and leave it at that."

Sienna brushes her fingertips along my forearm before she pulls me back to her. "I never thought of you as the jealous type. I have to admit I'm a little surprised, and not only because it's downright presumptuous of you to expect me to wait forever and be alone that whole time."

As much as I want to control my temper, I can't stop myself from asking, "So does he rock your world, or is this just another guy like the others?"

She looks past me, unable to meet my gaze when she answers, "I can't compare every man to you for the rest of my life. I'd be alone forever then. You know that, so it's cruel to even ask such a thing."

Good. I want her to do just that every time she meets someone new. I want her to compare everyone to me because I do the same thing every time I meet a woman.

It's the reason there's been no one since Sienna.

"Did you keep your promise not to kidnap any other women? I hope so because you're not good at it," she says with a hint of a smile, still not able to face me.

I move toward her, loving the feel of her body pressed against mine when I stop right in front of her. "I haven't kidnapped any women. I swear. I haven't been with anyone since you, hostage or not."

My confession comes out far more serious than I

intended, and finally, she turns her head to look at me. "You haven't been with anyone for the past two years?" she asks in amazement.

With a shrug, I try to play off my celibacy. "It's not like I have time to be seducing women. I'm a killer. That's a full-time job."

Every word of that other than my being a killer is a lie. Killing people is my job, but it's not like it's something that takes up most of my time. For the past two years, what I've done mostly is think about Sienna back on the island.

"Stop acting like it's nothing. You just told me you haven't slept with anyone else since we were together two years ago. Is that the truth?" Sienna asks with eyes full of disbelief.

"I don't have the time to go around bedding other beautiful women. Maybe if I had the time, but you know how it is."

She shakes her head and sighs. "Always with the cavalier attitude. I don't believe you anyway. There's no way a man like you hasn't been with even a single woman in two years."

We stare into one another's eyes while she waits to hear the truth from me. I'm not lying, though. I've met my fair share of women in the past couple years. Some I even considered sleeping with. But I didn't.

When someone has your heart, it's next to impossible to forget that or them.

Sienna's eyes grow big, and she asks, "Why? Why did you consign yourself to being alone? You owed me nothing. If anything, I owe you. You saved me and gave me the chance to have a life away from my family. I know Helix only did all of this for me because of you. Why wouldn't you find happiness with someone, even if it was only for a night, since you chose to not come to me?"

"I didn't want anyone else. Plus, I'm busy," I say, again pretending I'm so preoccupied with work that I don't have a few spare minutes in my days or nights to sleep with someone.

"Stop acting like this!" she cries, slapping me across the face. "Stop making it seem like it wasn't important!"

Her anger surprises me for a moment. I open my mouth to make another lame attempt at a joke, but I've got nothing. She wants honesty? Okay. She's going to get it.

"What do you want me to say? That I couldn't stop thinking about you and the thought of being with another woman left me feeling empty? That I wanted to come see you and feel whole again? That I've come back here to Connecticut to be sure you're okay so many fucking times that I could probably fly the plane myself I know the route so goddamned well? It wasn't important that I didn't sleep with someone in all that time. I couldn't because all I could think of was you."

Her mouth drops open, and for a second or two, I think she's about to cry. Instead, she pulls me to her and kisses me like I've fantasized about every day we've been apart. I take her in my arms, desperate to show her how much I've missed her.

Words aren't enough. She needs to feel it.

God, she tastes as sweet as she did back in Italy. That place where we spent those hours together is thousands of miles away, but I still would swear I can smell a hint of lemons surrounding her just like it did back there.

Our tongues tease how much we want one another. My cock stiffens until it nearly hurts pressing against my pants, and with each time she brushes against it, all I want to do is push her against the wall and bury myself inside her.

When she pulls away, I stagger back at how incredible one kiss could be. "That's some welcome kiss."

Looking down between us, she tugs my shirt out of my pants. "Feeling like living room sex or bedroom sex today?"

I don't answer her and slide my hands under her ass to lift her up. "I admit I'm looking forward to burying myself inside you, but I feel like I want more than just that tonight, so let's go with the bed."

As I carry her to her bedroom, she tightens her legs around my waist and grins like a woman with a plan. "What's that look for?" I ask.

"I don't know what look you mean, unless you're referring to how I can't wait to have you on top of me again."

Setting her down onto the bed, I don't give her a

chance to say anything more before I slide up her body to kiss away any words. The time for talking is over.

Sienna quickly strips out of her shirt and pants as I get rid of my clothes. I return to the only place in the world I want to be and kiss her again, loving the feel of her hands caressing my back. I'm rock hard and press my cock against her pussy, feeling the evidence of how ready she is for me.

When she drags her fingernails across the skin at the base of my spine, I push my hips forward. She opens her legs wide, but I don't plunge into her yet. I want to revel in this moment for a few seconds more.

But she seems to want to move faster as she scrapes her nails up the length of my back and buries her hands in my hair, tugging just a little to let me know kissing is all well and good, but what's pressing against her needy clit is what she really wants right now.

I lean away, tearing my mouth from hers, and look down at her. "Someone's in a hurry."

She runs her fingertips down over my chest and answer, "Not a hurry. Just interested in the good stuff that you keep rubbing against me. I'd call that teasing, by the way, in case you're wondering."

God, I've missed that sass that's so much a part of her. "You want teasing? Oh, I can tease with the best of them. Looks like you might never get what you want now."

Even though I'm not serious, she slides her hand

between us to where my erect cock sits waiting for some attention and wraps her fingers around it. "No more teasing, Alaric. I've waited two years for you. It's cruel to make me wait any longer."

Every touch of her hand on me makes me wince and moan. "No more crueler than my having to wait all that time for you."

She's making it very hard for me to not just go balls to the wall and fuck her like I've fantasized about every night since I last saw her. I want to show Sienna I missed more of her than her pussy, but each time she runs her hand down my shaft, I want to say fuck it and rip her underwear off to bury my cock in that perfect cunt of hers.

"I think you have your definition of tease confused with something else."

Sienna cups my balls and gives them a tiny squeeze, and that's all I can take. She wants to jump right in. She's going to get that and more.

I hook my thumb in the bottom of her underwear and rip, tearing the things off her left leg. Somehow, she's surprised and looks down at the torn fabric like she didn't basically tell me to do exactly that.

"And I'm the one in a hurry? You didn't see me tearing your underwear off your body."

As I tug the remnants of her panties down her other leg to toss them onto the floor, I chuckle. "Feel free. I have no problem going commando."

I take care of the last bit of my clothes before she can try to do to me what I just did to her, and a second later, we're both naked. Sienna returns her hands to my cock, but the time for stroking and teasing is over.

Pushing them away from my body, I roll onto my back and pull her on top of me. She's wet and ready, and since she didn't want to bother with any more foreplay, I don't waste any time sliding my cock into her willing body.

She sits up, giving me the perfect angle to hit right where I want to in her tight cunt. I set my hands on her hips and force her down the last inch or so until I'm all the way in.

With a smile, she says, "I feel like that went from zero to sixty in just a few seconds. I hope you aren't disappointed that I didn't want to wait."

I lift my hips off the mattress and drive into her body. "Not sure how I could be disappointed considering where I get to be now. So what do you say you be a good girl and ride my cock to show me how much you wanted this?"

"Good girl?" she says, mocking me with my own words while she takes every inch of me down to my balls. "And what does that mean?"

Hiking her up off my cock until only the head is still in her, I smile. "It means I'll let go of your hips and you ride me. Ready?"

I sense she wants something else, but that can happen later. For now, I want to stare up at her beautiful face as she gets off on my cock.

Sienna sets her hands on my chest and leans down

to kiss me sweetly, whispering against my lips, "I'm ready."

The second I release my hold on her, she goes to town. Rolling her hips and bucking on me, she gives my cock a ride like it's never had before. She's so wet and so tight that it feels like her cunt is going to strangle me down to my balls, but I can't get enough of how perfect she is around me.

The first round doesn't take long to get us both off, and when her orgasm hits her, she shudders and collapses onto my chest. I keep pumping into her, and a few seconds later, I fill her with all I have. Two years is a long time to wait for a release like this.

Sweaty and still trembling, she kisses next to my ear. "Oh, God, that felt so good. Sorry I didn't want to wait. It's been a long time that I've been waiting for you."

I slide out of her and wrap my arms around her drenched back. "No need to apologize. I've never met a man who didn't love having a woman want exactly what he wanted."

Lifting her head off my shoulder, she looks down into my eyes and frowns. "But you were all about the foreplay. I feel like I was a little bit pushy."

"Never think you have to be anything but who you are with me, Sienna. You wanted me to fuck you, and you told me that. Nothing wrong with being straightforward."

Her cheeks turn red with a blush that seems wrong

after what we just did. "I guess considering the way we started out, coy isn't exactly the way I should be."

"Coy, straightforward, whichever way you are, be yourself. That's all I ask."

A mischievous look fills her eyes, and she quietly says, "Then if I wanted to do it a certain way, all I'd have to do is ask?"

I know what she wants. It's been two long years, but I haven't forgotten how much she loved when I took her from behind.

A tiny suspicion about who she's been with in that time and what she's done with them creeps into my head, but I push it away before it grows into jealousy. What Sienna did and who she was with in that time is none of my business. She had every right to keep living after our time in Italy was over.

Even if I didn't. And even if I want to kill every man who's touched her since then.

I flip her onto her stomach in one smooth motion. Nudging my still hard cock against her ass, I lean down and whisper in her ear, "I know what you want. You don't have to ask."

For a moment, jealousy overwhelms me when she pushes back against me. Has she been like this with other men? Did they enjoy how much she loves being fucked like this?

But I can't think like that. I have no right to. I knew where she was the entire two years. I could have gone to her. She had a right to live her life.

"Alaric? Is something wrong?" she asks, turning her head to look back at me.

"No," I lie, wishing things could be different with her.

Wishing I could be different than the man I am.

"Up on your knees, baby. Let me give what you want."

She obeys without hesitation, even wiggling her ass against me to show how much she wants me to fuck her this way. Thankfully, my cock doesn't have the same tendency for jealousy that my mind has, so he's hard and ready to go.

I glide through her wet pussy and pull back. Jealousy takes me over, and I slide my hand around her throat, squeezing as I ask in her ear, "Still thinking you can't take me in your ass?"

There's no reason to ask that. I know it, and still I can't stop myself. And what the hell am I going to do with that information when she gives it to me? What the fuck is wrong with me?

She takes a sharp breath in when I let my fingers trail down the crack of her ass, and I know the answer before she says a word. Somehow, the fact that she hasn't been with anyone like that makes me feel good. It's messed up and I have no fucking right to expect her to not let herself feel pleasure just because I'm not someone who should be in her life, but there it is.

"Alaric, no. Nothing. There, I mean."

"Nothing?" I ask, unable to stop the question

before it leaves my lips. Jesus, I'm a glutton for punishment.

Sienna shakes her head and stares into my eyes. "No, nothing. Not a finger, and certainly not any man's dick. Nothing."

What a possessive ass I am, on top of being fucked up.

Hiding all that's going on inside me, I run my finger up her drenched slit and pull it back toward her ass. It slides in and she makes a noise that sounds like a tiny cry. Before she can protest, I fill her cunt completely. That gets me a gasp.

"Oh, God...I don't know what it is about that, but it feels so good."

I watch her grasp at the sheets as I pump into her and groan, "Which? My cock or my finger?"

Sienna shakes her head wildly, practically sobbing out her answer. "I don't know."

Jesus, she's perfect taking me this way, and for a fleeting second, I think about seeing how she'd like the real thing in her ass. I dismiss that thought immediately, though. I didn't exaggerate when I told her it would take longer than we have for her to be able to handle me like that.

Even more, I've already been a possessive fuck. I don't have to be a complete shithead with her.

Over and over, I pump into her, inching her toward another orgasm. I feel her body begin to surrender to me. Sienna whimpers as her release gets close, pushing back against my cock and my finger for more.

"That's it, baby. Let yourself go. I want to feel that pretty cunt of yours milk my cock like I know it can."

Her arms shoot out in front of her, and a few seconds later, she slams back against me as her entire body convulses. The feel of her cunt squeezing my cock and her asshole tightening against my thumb sends my body into overdrive, and I pound into her, fucking her with abandon. She takes every thrust, moaning loudly into the pillow as I piston my cock in and out in search of my own release.

When it happens, I feel like the top of my head is going to blow off for a second, but then I pump into her for one final time, filling her body with all I have. The backs of my legs hurt like I've run a fucking marathon, but I've never felt so good in my life.

Sienna collapses onto the bed, and I follow her, exhausted and utterly satisfied like never before. I let out a heavy sigh and slide my arm around her waist to pull her to me.

"That was incredible," she says softly as she nuzzles my neck.

"We are pretty good when it comes to that," I say, smiling as I watch her wind her legs around my body like a vine around a tree branch.

She has a way of wrapping a person up in her and not just physically.

As I think that, she lifts her head off my shoulder and pushes her hair back. "How long can you stay?"

I wish I could say forever. I wish I could say as long as she wants me to. I can't do either, though. This, like Italy, can't last.

Even though I wish more than anything it could.

"I'll be here until you fall asleep."

A slow smile lights up her face. "Then I'm going to stay up all night."

I kiss her and wish we could have every night from now on together. But it can't be. Who I am won't allow that.

When she puts her head on my chest and lets out a tiny sigh, I know it won't be long before she'll be asleep, and our time will be over.

At least for tonight.

Keeping to the shadows near the hedges that run along the driveway, I glance up at the main house and see no lights on now. At least I won't be running into anyone I don't want to see.

A second after that thought enters my brain, I hear a someone behind me say in a gruff voice, "The prodigal son returns."

Fuck. Even after all these years away from this place, I'd recognize that voice anywhere.

I turn around to see my older brother standing on the driveway with a smug look on his face. As always. Someday, I'm going to remove that fucking smirk permanently.

"Sebastian," I say flatly, unable to muster anything but disgust for this turn of events.

Of all the people I hoped not to run into tonight, he's near the top of the list. Maddox Rule would be first, but his favorite son runs a close second.

"Still sneaking around and getting in trouble? I swear you've never grown up, Alaric. Mason and Stephen act older than you. Fuck, Ava and Gabrielle act more mature."

"Right. Well, this has been a little slice of heaven, but I need to go."

As I turn to walk away, he says, "You come all this way and you won't even bother to say hello to your mother and father?"

Every word comes out of his mouth more irritating than the last one, so by the time he finishes, all I want to do is inflict some kind of pain on him. He knows damn well why I have no interest in seeing our father. As for our mother, that's a different story, but unfortunately, Willow Rule never comes alone.

Only as a set with Maddox, and that I can do without.

A pang of guilt hits me for a moment that now Sebastian will tell her I was here. I can't be bothered with that. I need to push that away like everything else about this place.

"She'll be fine. I'm sure she'll hear all about it from you."

"You know, I get hating Dad, but what did Mom ever do to you? Actually, I don't get hating Dad. What the hell did he or any of us ever do to make you turn your back on your family?"

Laughter explodes out of me, almost as if I can't stop myself. "I didn't turn my back on the Rules. I just went to the one Rule who understands me."

Sebastian huffs in disgust. "A fucking criminal who had to run away to escape spending the rest of his life in prison. What's it take to understand poor Alaric? The mind of a psychopath?"

Asshole. Like he has any right to be tagging anyone with the criminal slur. He and our father are nothing more than that. They just hide their illegal actions behind the guise of business.

"Whatever, Sebastian. Enjoy living your life in that ivory tower courtesy of our last name. It's a perfect place for you."

When I turn to walk away, he shoves me, and that's all it takes. I spin around and lunge at him, taking him to the ground. I always did like beating up on my big brother. Around my size, he never had to fight his way through life because everyone treated him like something fucking special because he's Maddox Rule's firstborn son.

I, on the other hand, have the same DNA and last name, yet I never got the free pass he did. So I learned to fight while he learned to charm. Tonight, he's going to feel the pain of what my past is like.

He catches me on the jaw once, but I slam my fist into his face twice, stunning him. Blood pours from his nose, even though I don't think it's broken. He might be able to take a shot better if he had to practice every day of his life.

"What's going on? Sebastian, who is this? I'm calling the police!"

Hoping to avoid getting cops involved, I quickly jump off Sebastian, leaving him bloody and beaten on the ground. When my mother sees my face, she staggers back a few steps.

Nothing like being visited by a ghost from the past.

"Alaric? Is that really you?" she asks after staring at me for a few seconds.

When I don't answer, she asks, "Why were you attacking your brother?"

Sebastian grumbles something about me being an asshole before standing up, his hands covering his nose still gushing blood. "I think it's time security escorted this trespasser out."

"You will do no such thing! This is your brother, and no matter what you two were arguing about, he is as welcome at this house as any of us are."

My brother sulks after being put in his place and walks away toward the house, probably to go run to our father. Fucking fantastic.

"Are you back? I mean, for good?" my mother asks.

I've never been good, so that's not a logical question. Then again, Willow Rule would never be confused with someone who's logical.

"No. I can't stay here."

My answer doesn't seem to register with her, and

she rushes toward me to take me in her arms. "I've missed you so much, Alaric. I've wished for this every day since you left. Please stay. We haven't seen you in so long."

I shake my head as the words I need to stay get trapped in my throat. Maddox Rule I could crush with no feeling whatsoever. Willow Rule is a different story.

Gently, I push her away and see tears on her cheeks. "This isn't where I belong anymore."

"This is your home," she says with sadness clinging to every word.

She knows better.

"Not anymore."

She reaches out to touch me, and when her fingers graze my forearm, it's like every good memory I have of us comes over me like a tidal wave. If only it was just the two of us.

Looking up at me with those big blue eyes that never fail to make me want to make her happy, she tries to smile but fails. "This will always be your home, and we will always be your family, Alaric. Nothing can change that."

I love her, but my mother lives in a world that doesn't exist anymore.

"I have to go."

As I walk away, she says, "Please stay. I want you to."

I take one last look back at her and smile. "I have to go. Don't worry about me. I'm fine."

"I'll always worry about you, honey. You're my son. I don't care how old you get. I'll always worry."

Anyone else on the planet could say something like that and it wouldn't affect me like it does coming from her. I need to get away from here. It was a mistake coming back. I should have known I couldn't come home. I don't belong in this place. Maybe I never did.

"Alaric. Please," she says sadly, but I simply shake my head as I disappear into the darkness.

I can't feel like this again.

CHAPTER FOUR

ienna

THE SOUND OF MY PHONE CHIMING THAT MYSTICAL tune wakes me up, and I look around for Alaric, even though I know better. He said he'd be here until I fell asleep, and as much as I wanted to never close my eyes again, I drifted off sometime after our third round of sex.

I look over at my nightstand and grab my phone, answering it without even checking who it might be. "Hello?"

"Sabrina, did you sleep in today? It's nearly nine already," Trent says with more than a hint of disapproval in his tone.

He's very much a man who likes to keep to schedules, and since I'm usually up long before this time on most days, I guess it's not surprising he's wondering if I've channeled my inner sloth this morning. His straight-and-narrowness is one of the things I like most about him, actually. He's nothing like my family or a certain person named after a famous barbarian.

Until last night, I'd convinced myself that was a good thing. Now I'm not so sure.

Sitting up in bed, I stretch my limbs and answer him. "I guess I must have. It's okay. Nine isn't really that late."

"What did you do last night?" Trent asks, and instantly, guilt washes over me.

"Nothing. Nothing at all. Just hung out for a while. I was supposed to go with the girls, but I begged off. This graduation stuff is exhausting. You know how it is."

The words come rushing out of my mouth like I can't stop them. I know I sound like I'm covering something up, so I quickly add, "So, are we going to see each other today?"

"That's what I'm calling about. Get up because I have something special planned. You have the whole day free, right? That's what you told me last week."

I slide out of bed and walk over toward my dresser to grab the underwear and bra I'll wear today. "Yeah. All day. What do you have planned?" I ask, never thrilled with surprises.

My entire life has shown me that surprises are rarely as wonderful for the person being surprised as the one doing the surprising. All those people my father and brothers surprised over the years would agree with me if they weren't six feet under.

Trent chuckles in that playful way I adore about him. "No more questions. Get ready and meet me at the train station in an hour."

The train station? Ooooh, maybe he's planning on taking me into Manhattan for a celebration lunch? Or maybe we're going to see a Broadway show.

My first instinct is to ask more questions, exactly what he told me not to do, but I clamp my mouth shut until the urge passes. "An hour it is. Where at the train station do you want me to meet you?"

"It doesn't matter. You'll see me as you're walking there. I'll be the one with the graduation present for my girlfriend."

Ooooh, a present too? I'd been wondering what Trent would do to celebrate my big day. I guess this is it. I better get a move on so I don't miss it all.

"Okay, an hour at the station. I don't know what you have planned, but this reminds me of those old movies you got me watching. Taking the train to some unknown destination to do God only knows what. Very old school, Trent. I love it!"

"Good, then get yourself ready. See you in an hour!"

"I'll be there."

"Love you," he says right before I end the call, just like he always does. And I never do.

"Mmmm-hmmm," I answer, unable to say those words back to him.

It's not that I don't care for Trent. I do. He's been one of the best parts of my senior year here at Yale. He treats me great, and when he does things like today where he surprises me with something sweet and thoughtful he's planned out, I really think I could love him.

But then the one truth that never goes away crashes into all those warm feelings I have for Trent and ruins everything. I'm in love with Alaric. I have been for two years, despite the fact that he never came around all that time. Last night proved to me that love never faded. If anything, it grew stronger.

So like I have since the first time Trent told me he loved me a few months ago, I smile and hum like the thought of his love pleases me. It doesn't displease me. It simply can't overcome my feelings for Alaric.

As I shower and get ready to meet Trent at the train station, I chastise myself for being stupid. What is that saying Natasha is always repeating? A bird in the hand is worth two in the bush? It's always sounded borderline perverted, but the way she explains things it means what you have is worth far more than what you wish you could have. That's how I should feel toward Trent. He's the bird in my hand, and Alaric is the possibility of two in some hedge somewhere.

I should value what I have instead of always wishing for something I know is a longshot. Still, even the mere thought of Alaric makes me question if I will ever be able to love anyone else.

Wrapping my wet hair in a towel, I close my eyes and think to myself how stupid I am. I've got a wonderful guy in Trent, and what do I do? I sleep with a man who kidnapped me. Yes, he's the reason I got away from my family, but the man ignored me for two years after that!

Christ, I need to get some perspective. So Alaric and I have incredible sex. That does not make a love match. So I feel special whenever I think of him. That and a couple bucks will get me a cup of coffee.

Trent is the man I should be focusing my attention on, not some ghost who shows up to haunt me every couple years.

Resolved to cherish what I have instead of hoping to have something that may never happen, I study my face in the mirror as I let my damp hair tumble out from under the towel. The reddish tint Ashley put in my hair is fading already, and it's only been three weeks. Time for a touch-up.

I better wear something really special since we're likely going into the city. As I head toward my bedroom, I weigh the choice of going with my navy-blue tank dress or my yellow sundress with the little blue flowers across the hem. Today feels like a yellow dress kind of day.

A half hour later, I take one last look in the full-length mirror on the back of my bedroom door and like what I see. I'm a little less tan than I'd like for the yellow dress, but other than that, I look ready for my big surprise.

On my way to the door, my phone rings. Fishing it out of my little purse that matches the color of those royal blue flowers on my dress, I see it's Trent. "Hey, I'm on my way. No need to worry that I fell back asleep," I joke.

"Just wanted to check. You didn't sound entirely with it before."

I laugh as I lock my front door and make my way toward the elevator. "And here I thought you trusted me. Do you know I think this is the first time you ever called to check that I'm on my way? This surprise must really be special."

"Oh, it is. See you in a few."

Now this is what a good boyfriend does for the woman he loves. He plans surprises to celebrate her big days. He checks up on her to make sure she's okay. He doesn't disappear for two years and then suddenly come around one night.

When I step out into the sunlight, I run my hand over my new cross and necklace. Alaric did keep my old one all this time. That was thoughtful and shows he thought about me while we've been apart.

And yet, I woke up alone in bed this morning. The choice is clear. I don't know why I'm making it more difficult than it needs to be.

I look up toward the perfect blue sky and smile. It's a gorgeous day for a surprise trip into the city. I really hope Trent got us tickets to that new show everyone's been talking about. Then again, it is such a beautiful day that a few hours in Central Park would be wonderful too.

He's standing near a doorway into the station, and I wave as I make my way toward him. This is how normal people behave when they care about each other. I have to remember that and forget any ridiculous romantic notions I have about Alaric because that's all they are. Silly ideas I should have grown out of already.

"Ready to tell me what this surprise is yet?" I ask with a smile when I reach Trent.

There's a wickedness in his expression that seems misplaced when he shakes his head and answers, "Just a few steps more."

That's odd. Is part of my surprise in the train station?

I walk through the doorway inside and feel Trent's hands on my shoulders. Glancing back, I notice him looking over my head, and when I turn around to see what he's focused on, something heavy hits me in the back of my skull. Before I can cry out, everything goes black.

EVERYTHING HURTS. THE BACK OF MY HEAD THROBS like a heartbeat back there. My shoulders feel like someone's spent hours squeezing them, and my legs feel like they're made of lead.

What happened to me? Did I pass out or have some kind of attack in the train station?

I slowly open my eyes to see I'm somewhere dark. A quick scan of the room shows me there are no windows here. Is this a room at the station? That would make sense because they wouldn't leave a woman who's passed out just sprawled out on the floor in front of other riders. If I'm somewhere in the train station, they have the heat cranked to somewhere close to ninety because it's unbelievably hot in here.

My mouth tastes like old cotton mixed with dirt. Did I have my mouth open when I fell? Where is Trent? Shouldn't he be here with me to make sure I'm not alone when I wake up?

I move to straighten myself and sit up, and that's when I feel something pulling on my arms. Barely cognizant of my surroundings, I instantly know this sensation. I've felt it before.

Looking down, I see my arms tied to the wooden arms of an old chair. Son of a bitch! Why the fuck am I being restrained? Something tells me it's not the fine folks at Amtrak keeping me tied up here.

When I try to move my legs, I find my ankles have been tied to the legs of the chair. For a second or two, I let myself hope that this is Alaric's doing and somehow he thinks this little stunt is cute or romantic. It's not, but men think dumb things sometimes.

"Hello? Who's there? Why am I tied up in here? Please someone tell me what's going on!" I yell as loud as my parched throat will allow me.

No one answers, and as I wait a minute or two before I try again, I study the room around me as best I can. It's dark, but there's light coming in from under the door about eight feet in front of me. It makes seeing my surroundings slightly easier, but all I recognize is that this is a room with no windows and only this chair I'm tied to.

Why is it so hot in here?

This isn't Alaric's doing. Something is very wrong.

I try once again to make someone hear me, but my mouth is so dry that I can only cry out a few words before the rest get trapped in my throat. My attempt at making some saliva turns out to be fruitless too.

Fully awake, I try to get my arms and legs out of these fucking restraints, but it's no use. Pulling and tugging only makes the ropes dig into my skin, so by the time I finish trying to escape, all I have is raw wrists and ankles to show for my effort.

Suddenly, the door opens, and I stare into the face of a man I don't recognize. I study his expression as he steps into the room and shudder.

He's not here to help me.

"Please let me out of these restraints," I croak out. "Who are you? Why am I here? Where is Trent?" I ask into the silence of the room as the man stares down at me in disgust.

"Matteo was right. You ask too many questions. Shut your mouth and behave and maybe this won't hurt too much."

I look up at him in horror. "Matteo? Is he behind this? Why?"

"This is going to hurt a lot if you don't shut your mouth."

"What won't hurt too much? Because if you're talking about these ropes, they already hurt. Why are you keeping me hostage here?"

He ignores my questions just as he's ignored my pleas to release me, but I keep asking, even as every ounce of moisture in my mouth and throat threatens to dry up. "Please let me go. I'm no one. Trust me. My name is Sabrina, and I'm a simple college student."

A vicious laugh explodes out of the man's face, frightening me. "Sabrina? Did you come up with that? Because we both know that's not your name, Sienna. Now just sit tight and you'll see what's going on in a little while."

When he steps close to me, I stare up into his face and try to see if I know this person since he clearly knows me. He's no one I've ever met. Anger seems to be chiseled into his features. Dark hair with a touch of gray at the temples tells me he's older than my brothers.

"Who are you? Why are you keeping me here?" I ask, expecting answers to neither of my questions.

The man surprises me, though. "My name is Lucius. Don't worry. We'll get to know each other very well soon enough. For now, sit there and behave, Sienna. You don't want me to have to punish you for not being a good girl, do you?"

My mouth drops open at the way he talks to me like I'm some rebellious child he feels the need to scold. "Good girl? I'm not your daughter, so don't pull that good girl shit on me. There's only one man I tolerate that from, and you aren't him."

He narrows his eyes, and then a moment later, he thrusts his hand forward, wrapping his fingers around my neck. Lucius squeezes tightly, cutting off my airway instantly. I shake my head to force him to stop, but it's no use.

"Now behave, or I swear that I'm going to have to hurt you."

His dark eyes stare into mine, terrifying me, but I don't close my eyes or look away. He won't get the benefit of my fear now or ever. Whoever this fucker is, I won't back down from him.

When he loosens his grip on my throat, I say, "You can do whatever you want to me, but I'm not some frightened little thing. I'm Sienna Rossetti, and if you don't know what that means, that's your misfortune."

He leans down so his face is directly in front of mine, and I see just how much older he is than I am. Tiny wrinkles fan out from the corners of his dark eyes, probably from a lifetime worth of squinting angrily at people, and the lines around his mouth say he's been unhappy more than a few times.

"Good to hear you know who you are, Sienna. I like that," he says in a low voice.

"If my brother is behind this, be sure to tell him I won't forget the fact that he had me taken and tied up like this. The last member of my family who thought it was a good idea to hurt me found out what happens when you do that. Maybe you should remind him of that fact," I whisper, unable to raise my voice because I'm so parched.

That gets me a big, evil grin from Lucius. "Oh, we're going to have a good time, you and me."

He slides his forefinger along my jaw, and I turn my head in disgust. "Don't touch me. I'm not yours to touch."

Stuffing his hand into my hair, he tugs my head back hard, bringing tears to my eyes. "Not yet. All in good time. Now behave yourself, Sienna, or your brother will be the least of your problems."

Lucius releases his hold on my hair, but not until he yanks my head back one more time. As he turns to leave the room, I ask, "What did you do to Trent? Where is he?"

Without looking back at me, he answers, "Trent did the job he was hired for, and now he's enjoying some well-earned time off."

Job he was hired for? What does that mean?

"What are you saying?"

He chuckles low and deep and spins around to face me. "What it means is he had one job, and he did that job well. Didn't you ever wonder how he seemed to appear out of nowhere, Sienna? One day Trent Michaels doesn't exist, and the next, he's the perfect man who's madly in love with you? That never set off any alarm bells? Come on, now. You're a Rossetti. You should have known better than to trust a perfect stranger like that. You had to know we'd be coming to get you. You were never going to live some happily ever after life in America. Trent was there to make sure when the time came that you returned to where you belong. Welcome home, Sienna."

Home? As in Italy? My brother and this goon of his brought me back here? Why? What good could I serve Matteo now?

I don't bother to ask Lucius since I highly doubt he'll give me any straight answers. I'll wait until I see that son of a bitch of a half-brother of mine to ask my questions. For now, all I want to do is cry at the news that Trent turned out to be as suspicious as Alaric said he was.

But this asshole standing in front of me won't get the pleasure of seeing my tears. He's right. I need to keep in mind just who the hell I am.

I'm Sienna Rossetti, and I've done this whole kidnapping and tied to a chair thing before. I got out then, and I'll get out now.

As the door to the room closes, I tilt my head back and take a deep breath. *Alaric, wherever you are, come find me and help me fuck these bastards up for thinking they should take me from my happy life.*

I can only hope our time together isn't over yet.

CHAPTER FIVE

laric

AFTER A LONG TRIP BACK TO THE ISLAND, I SIT ON the edge of my bed and roll my shoulders to release the tension. Another job done and now my time is my own. That's why I like this deal I have with Helix. While his other men are sent out on assignments when he gets a request to take care of someone, I only kill for him.

Thankfully, there aren't many people in this world he wants to disappear.

I reach into my pants pocket and touch Sienna's gold cross. Closing my eyes, I try to imagine what she's doing right now. Late afternoon on a Sunday. She's probably hanging out with her friends. Maybe heading into town to go shopping.

Or maybe she's with that asshole boyfriend of hers. Trent. That's a douchebag name if I've ever heard one.

Before last night, it had been months since I last got up there to check on her. Even though Helix has his guys watching her, I like seeing for myself that she's okay.

She looked different than the woman I knew in Italy. She's still the same Sienna, though.

The time before last night, she almost caught me following her when she and her friends went to Little Italy in New Haven. I got too close, and I think she caught a glimpse of me before I ducked into a pizza place. I watched through the glass window of that restaurant as she looked around like she knew she was being spied on and wondered if she thought it might be me.

As much as I hated being back in Connecticut, I loved being so close to her. It was sheer torture not being able to talk to her and hear her voice again, but that's not something I can do.

Or should even want to do. Not with who I am and what my life is like.

Sliding her cross out of my pocket, I place it in the center of my palm and study it. The gold looks duller than usual today. Probably too much rubbing against my thigh since I had to do so much goddamned walking to find that guy last night.

I lift it up and brush it against my shirt right over my heart before studying it again to see if it shines like it should. A glint of light from the late afternoon sun outside hits it, and I smile. As good as when she gave it to me.

The necklace she wore it on broke just a few months after that night in the villa, but I always carry this cross with me. It's like I get to have part of her with me at all times.

Sentimental and stupid. That's all it probably is. Still, every morning when I wake up, I look for the gold cross on my dresser as I'm getting dressed.

I slide it into my pocket and lean back on the bed to stare up at the ceiling in my room. I should have made sure I stayed to go to her graduation. I've known for months when it will be held.

No, that's not something I should do. I don't belong nearby on her big day. She deserves to enjoy her moment without wondering if someone's watching from the bushes, and as much as I can follow anyone else in the world without having them know, I want to get too close to her. That makes me sloppy.

I smile at the thought of her in her cap and gown looking beautiful and accomplished surrounded by all the other Yale graduates. Congratulations, Sienna. You did it.

MY PHONE VIBRATING AGAINST MY HIP ROUSES ME from my daydreams about her, and I lift it up in front of my eyes to see who's calling. Focusing, I see it's

Helix. Odd. He usually doesn't bother me with work after the sun goes down.

I scrub the last of my nap away and head down to his office. Maybe someone pissed him off royally and he wants me to do a job ASAP. That's not really Helix's style, though.

As I pass through the entryway into the other side of the house, I see Kerry on her way upstairs. She smiles and points toward the hallway to her husband's office. "He's burning the midnight oil tonight. I think something big is happening back home."

Back home? The plot thickens. Even more curious now, I pick up my pace.

Helix is standing near the window in his office that looks out toward the pool area. He doesn't look particularly perturbed about anything, so maybe this is just him wanting to get a jump on tomorrow's work.

"What's up?"

When he turns to face me, I see a hint of something different in his expression. Maybe worry? I quickly decide it has nothing to do with any of his own kids since Kerry wasn't upset, but if it has to do with back in the States, that means one of my cousins is in trouble.

Or maybe one of my siblings? Or my mother?

"Sit down, Alaric. I want to talk to you."

As I do as he orders, I joke, "Sounds serious. Something happen to make the world turn upside down?"

When he walks behind his desk, he continues to

stand, which confuses me even more. What the hell is going on?

"Something's happened."

I wait for him to continue, and when he doesn't, I ask, "With?"

"With the situation back in Connecticut," he answers in a serious voice, frowning.

Fear races through me. "Who? Is it my mother?"

She looked okay the other night I was at the estate. Unhappy I wouldn't stay but still healthy like always. What could have happened?

Helix shakes his head, and a smile replaces the look of unhappiness from a moment ago. "No. Why would you think that?"

A headache begins forming at the base of my skull from all this spoon-feeding bullshit he's doing. "Because you said something's happened with the situation back in Connecticut and you look downright concerned. Since neither of us is crazy about my father, I figured it had to do with my mother. So would you mind just cutting to the chase and telling me why the fuck you called me down here tonight?"

He takes his own sweet time sitting down and getting settled so I'm about to explode when he finally starts to explain what's going on. "Something's changed with Sienna."

My heart drops into my stomach at the sound of her name and the words *something's changed*. "What? What's changed? She's graduating. Is that it?"

I sound distinctly unlike me right now. It's like I

can't stop my voice from ratcheting up higher and higher as I speak, and all I want to do is shut up. But I can't.

"Is that what you mean? Do you want to send her a card with a nice big fat check? Why are you telling me anything about her?"

As always, he's calm and merely shakes his head as I start to ramble. "Because you care about her. Stop acting like a dick."

Even as my heart continues to race, I take a deep breath in and blow it out of my lungs in the hope that I can relax. Something's happened with Sienna. That's not good. If it was merely about her graduation, Helix wouldn't be bothering to even mention it to me.

Something's changed means something bad happened.

"So what's changed?" I ask, unsure I want to know the answer.

"You know, I don't think I've ever seen so much of your father in you until tonight. It's not a good look on you. That's for sure."

His mention of my father sets me off, but I'm not in the right headspace to fight with Helix tonight. I stand to leave, preferring to walk away if he doesn't want to tell me what the hell has happened. Fuck him. I can fly up there and find out on my own. It's not like he's the only way I can learn about what's going on with Sienna.

Just before I walk out of his office, he says, "Her

brother found out where she is. He sent someone to get her."

His words stop me cold. Is he telling me she's dead?

Without turning around, I ask, "What happened?"

I stare at the turquoise blue and green turtle mosaic hanging on the wall in the hallway outside his office as the seconds tick by and he doesn't answer my simple question. All he needs to do is tell me what the fuck happened to her. Why is that so difficult?

Finally, I turn around and stare at him, still confused why the hell he hasn't answered me. "If she's dead, just fucking say it. I'm not a boy, Helix. I can handle hearing someone's dead. For Christ sake, I make people dead, so it's not like I'm a stranger to the circumstance."

"She's not dead. From what I hear, she's very much alive."

"Then why drag her back to Italy? Does he miss having her around the table for Sunday dinners?"

Helix frowns like what he has to say disgusts him. "Guess again. Big brother's not happy his sister gave the family the slip, so he's making sure she pays for that and stays put forever."

I take a step back into his office and shake my head. "What does that mean?"

"It means I'm sure he's got plans for her. You know how families can be, Alaric."

I roll my eyes at that thought. "I do, all too well. So

if he's not planning on killing her, what's her punishment going to be?"

Helix shakes his head. "No clue yet. Gideon will know more about this when you get to him. I'm guessing, though, that his retribution will have something to do with keeping her in Italy from this point on."

"So she loses her freedom and that's the best she can hope for? Her brother's a real asshole, isn't he?"

"I'd say so."

"So there's nothing you can do to help her?" I ask, picturing Sienna forced onto a plane to Italy at gunpoint.

"I didn't say that, now did I?"

Jesus, I swear to God he's either getting charged by the syllable tonight, or he's enjoying this torture he's working on me. "Where is she, Helix?"

"Back home on the Amalfi Coast. They grabbed her this morning. I have Gideon keeping his ear to the ground to find out where, but for right now, I have no idea specifically where they're holding her."

"Fuckers. I swear to God I'm going to make every single person in her goddamned family who had something to do with this dead," I mumble under my breath, barely able to contain my rage.

"Take the plane. Go find her and get her away from there before they do something like marry her off like it's the Middle fucking Ages over there," Helix says, still so calm.

I nod and take a deep breath to calm myself. "Thanks. Not that it's going to change my mind, but is there any reason I shouldn't wipe out every fucking brother she has that's involved in this shit they pulled?"

A slow smile turns up the corners of Helix's mouth. "None that I can see. They know how this works. They made their play. Now we make ours. Coordinate with Gideon when you get to Italy. I've had him watching the Rossettis and their friends for a while. He'll have more information by the time you arrive."

"Okay. I'll go now. I swear to God, if they hurt her…"

I can't finish that sentence. She better not have a single beautiful hair on her head out of place when I find her, or I'm going to lose my fucking mind. What happens next will be all they deserve.

"Just get over there and find her. Oh, by the way, just for good measure, it was the boyfriend who turned on her."

Fucking Trent. I knew he couldn't be trusted.

"I thought you checked him out. You said he was okay."

"He became not okay. They must have gotten to him."

The headache that began at the base of my skull now encompasses my entire head. "Fucking asshole. I knew he was no good."

I don't wait for Helix to tell me my gut reaction to him was probably jealousy and not some real knowledge of how bad he was. I know what I felt. Jealous or not, I knew he was bad.

Just for that, I'm going to fucking kill him too if I see him.

CHAPTER SIX

laric

THE VILLA AURELIA SPARKLES LIKE A NEW PENNY, impressing even me as I walk through the front doors to Gideon's hotel. In truth, it's Helix's since he handles all the hotels he owns, but this one is his younger son's responsibility, and I have to say he stepped up to the challenge.

Not that the place was a run-down slum when he got control of it, but his work over the past two years has made it one of the premier destinations on the Amalfi Coast. He stands at the foot of the grand marble staircase in the center of the main lobby looking pleased as I make my way toward him.

Much like his father, Gideon cuts an impressive figure no matter where he is, but right now, he reminds me of some wealthy landowner overlooking his holdings with utter satisfaction. As tall as I am at six foot four, he wears a dark gray expensive Italian suit like always when he's in the view of the public here at the hotel. His dark hair and deep brown eyes are similar to mine, typical Rule family traits, but unlike me, he always appears so cool and calm every time I see him.

"Alaric, I thought you were getting here later this afternoon," he says with a smile as he extends his hand to shake mine.

"The pilot must have caught a tailwind or something because we made it to Naples in record time. The traffic on the drive here was the same as always, though. I don't miss that part of Italy when I leave. That's for sure."

I shake his hand and slap him on the back. "This place really has become impressive, Gideon. Is the chandelier in the middle of the lobby here new?"

He looks up at the ceiling and nods his appreciation. "The old one didn't have the same effect, so I had a craftsman come in and create something entirely unique to the hotel. It must be good if you noticed it. You're not exactly the kind of guy who pays attention to chandeliers."

That makes me laugh, but I need to focus on the job that's brought me here to the Amalfi Coast again. "Not generally. Your father told me you'd have some information that will help me find Sienna. Is there somewhere we can talk?"

Gideon's expression turns serious, and he points over toward the entrance to a conference room across the lobby. "We can discuss things freely in there."

Taking a seat at the end of the long conference table, I settle in to hear what he knows. I can never tell with Gideon if he has good news or bad news. He's far too icy most of the time to even hazard a guess.

He doesn't sit down, preferring to stand and lean against the wall as we talk. I don't know if it's that he doesn't like to relax at work or if he's always like this, but as I look at him positioned across the room from me now, I realize I've never seen him just kick back.

"So you know about Matteo Rossetti leading the family since you took the father out. That's been pretty much status quo for the past two years. Nothing big happened. He stepped into his father's place easily, it seems, and from what I hear, while he's not as well-loved as Salvatore, the son gets the job done and the Rossetti family is wealthier than ever."

I nod as Gideon goes through this introductory stuff I know most of and other details I don't care about. If Matteo and the rest of his family are making bank, I don't give a damn. As long as he left Sienna alone, I left them alone.

Now all that's changed.

"Good for them, I guess. What I want to know is if they brought Sienna back here and why."

Gideon winces, and I sense I'm about to hear bad news. Folding his arms across his chest, he says, "She's definitely here. Matteo couldn't stop himself from bragging the other day at his favorite restaurant. He told the entire place about how his sister was back in the fold and how happy he was."

"Why?" I ask, still not understanding what the point of dragging Sienna across the damned Atlantic was. "Is this just to make her life miserable and make sure she knows who's running the family now that Daddy's gone?"

"Not exactly. I've been hearing things since yesterday that tell me it's more than showing his sister who's boss. From what I'm told, the Rossetti family is planning a wedding."

My heart sinks at those words, but I ask, "Any chance it's Matteo or one of the other brothers who's getting married, and he wanted the entire family together?"

I know that's not the case. He's not going to kidnap Sienna just so she can be there when the happy couple lifts their champagne glasses in a toast to their nuptials.

With a shake of his head, Gideon dashes my hopes. "No. He intends on marrying her off to a man named Lucius Angeloni."

Now my heart skips a beat at the mere thought that Sienna is here for that reason. "Who the hell is he?"

"A friend of their father's. He's in his mid-fifties. From all I've heard, he's not a good choice for a husband. That's for sure."

A man twice her age? No, that's rarely a good

choice of a husband for a woman in her early twenties. The fact that she had to be kidnapped to be there to marry the guy makes him even a worse choice.

"Let me guess. Son of a bitch? Probably has a thing for being a shit to young women?" I ask, imagining this old asshole thinking he's gotten the golden ticket with Sienna.

"Well, let's put it this way. He's had a handful of women over the years. Nearly every one of them didn't make it out of the relationship with him alive."

"He has them killed?"

Jesus, Matteo Rossetti is even worse than I thought. I'm going to enjoy putting two into the back of that fucker's head.

Gideon corrects my mistaken assumption about Lucius Angeloni. "No, he does it himself. The old man likes it rough. Like really rough. His women get the worst of it. The last one was barely twenty. He beat the hell out of her, and rumor has it he gets off on it. She got away, so he's in the market for a new lady in his life."

"Sick fuck," I mumble, my stomach roiling at the image my mind's conjured up of Sienna at this asshole's mercy.

"Yeah. That's what's waiting for the future Mrs. Angeloni."

I stand up, my fingers gripping the table I'm so fucking angry right now. "Not if I have anything to do with it."

"So what's your plan?" Gideon asks with a hint more emotion than a moment before.

"I'll need a place to stay. Is the villa available?"

He shakes his head. "No. It's being refurbished and won't be done for another month."

Compared to Helix's other son, Alex, this one is practically a joy to deal with on most occasions. His desire for luxury is one part of him I could do without, though, especially now.

"Then I'll have to stay here," I say, hoping that makes him change his mind about the villa. No doubt, he won't want me running my business out of his hotel. He likes to keep it out of what Helix and I do most of the time. I'm sure he can get his designer back into the villa after I'm done with getting Sienna away from this place.

But he doesn't take the bait, strangely enough. "That's fine. I set aside one of the best rooms we have for you."

"The penthouse?" I ask with a chuckle, sure he didn't mean that.

Gideon's eyes get wide for a moment before he shakes his head. "Not likely since that's where I live. Not to worry, though. I made sure to give you a nice view."

I don't plan on enjoying the view much while I'm here. This trip is pure business. I need to find Sienna, get her the hell away from her family and that Lucius asshole, and disappear with her far away from here.

"Sasha has been briefed on your visit, so whatever you want, all you need to do is ask her."

His assistant, the tall, stunning blonde with icy blue eyes, there at my beck and call. It sounds good, but can I trust her?

"I need her to keep her mouth shut. Can she do that? If not, then she's no good to me."

He smiles like he's already thought about what he plans to do to her if she doesn't do exactly that. "Not to worry. She knows better than to say anything. That's why she's so valuable to me."

I've only met Sasha a handful of times, but every one of them made me question if she's more than an assistant to Gideon. She's beautiful, for sure, but he tends to go in for a different type than her.

Then again, who knows what happens when two people work as closely as they do, day in and day out?

"She needs to act like we don't know one another. Is acting one of her talents?"

His grin answers my question before he does. "Sasha does what she's told. That's why she's such a wonderful assistant. She'll do as I say. As for not telling anyone what you and I are up to, don't worry. That NDA she signed means she won't say a word."

Now I'm really unsure if they're more than just employer and employee. Curious, I ask, "Any chance there's another reason why she'll do as you tell her to?"

Gideon screws his face into a grimace for a moment before his icy expression returns. "Haven't you ever heard of not shitting where you eat? It's good advice. I try to follow it as often as permissible."

I laugh at how irritated my simple question made him. "So no extracurricular fun with your sexy assistant?"

He rolls his eyes and begins walking toward the door. "The last thing I want in my life is a woman just like me."

"That's technically not a no," I say as I follow him.

Gideon ignores my attempt to glean more information about what he does or doesn't do with his beautiful assistant. "Let's go so you can get into your room and get working on your job here."

That's one thing I can appreciate about Gideon. He's all business. At least he is with me. He doesn't let emotions get in the way of anything, and I like that. I've got enough on my plate dealing with what the hell I'm going to do to get Sienna away from her family and Lucius Angeloni.

CHAPTER SEVEN

ienna

HOURS SITTING IN THIS DARK ROOM WITHOUT A single person coming in to ask if I need food or water makes me feel like a real prisoner. My brother is a real piece of work doing this to me.

Not that I should be surprised. Our father put out a hit on me. Matteo's behavior isn't anywhere as bad as that. He probably thinks I'm going to collapse into a crying mess, but I'm stronger than that.

I may be a female, but I'm just as tough as he is. Even tougher, I think, because I've had to be. As a female in our family, it's not like I've been treated like a princess. My life has been far more of a fight against being held in places against my will than his ever was.

The same can be said for all my half-brothers.

They have no idea how to be strong because they never had to be. All they do is playact being strong. That's what happens when power is handed to you. You don't know how to fight for things.

But I do. Now Matteo and the rest of my family are going to find that out.

I try to move my arms, desperate to stretch my wrists after sitting here for God only knows how long, but unlike Alaric, whoever restrained me here meant business. My breath hitches in my chest at the thought of him. Does he know my brother took me? How could he since he probably went back to that island where he lives?

Then again, I've always had a feeling his uncle had people watching me, so maybe they do know I'm missing. The problem is I looked like I was merely walking to the train station to meet my boyfriend. It's possible no one saw me get taken away.

Trent. What a son of a bitch. All this time I thought he cared. He told me he loved me. I guess that was all a lie. I wonder if our entire time together was just a prelude to his handing me over to my brother, or did Matteo get to him and threaten to hurt him if he didn't help with his plan to drag me back here?

My mind quickly moves away from my good-for-nothing ex-boyfriend to the reason why I've been brought back here in the first place. What good do I do Matteo or anyone else in my family, for that matter? With my father gone, there's no reason to concern themselves with what's happening with me.

So why kidnap me and force me back here?

My head snaps up at the sound of the door opening, and in walks the man himself. Dressed in a black suit like always, Matteo looks so stereotypical gangster that I have to stifle a laugh when he flicks on the lightbulb above me. He truly has no idea how ridiculous he is.

"Time to come alive, Sienna. I thought I'd pay you a visit and explain just what's going to happen to you," he says, his accent much thicker than I remember.

Then again, Italian is his first language and he's never spent a day outside of this country, so I guess it's not surprising that he sounds like he does. Still, it serves to further make him more of a caricature than anything else.

"Matteo, how nice of you to come to see me. Nothing like kidnapping your sister and dragging her back to a life she clearly wanted to leave in the past."

For anyone else, I'd keep my attitude to a minimum, but my brother gets the full effect of how pissed I am at this situation. If he wanted nice, he should have left me alone to live my damn life back in the States.

"Stop being melodramatic," he says with a sneer. "You know this is how things are done in our family."

As if that makes it right. God, I hate him!

"So why did you do me the favor of bringing me back here? Wanted to give me an all-expense paid trip to the beautiful Amalfi Coast? Missed me so much you just had to see me again?"

Matteo reaches up and taps the lightbulb so it begins to swing like a pendulum above my head. With each pass, it creates ugly shadows on my brother's face that make him all the more hideous.

"You belong here, Sienna. Not living in America as some woman named Sabrina. You're a Rossetti, and no matter how much you wish that wasn't true, it is, so it's time you accept it."

What a ridiculous statement to make. As if being a Rossetti is something I should value or cherish. What the hell has that name or the family attached to it ever done for me?

"I belong where I want to be, not where you or any other of my brothers think I should go. This isn't the goddamned Middle Ages, Matteo. Women are allowed to decide their own fates. Even Italian women, the last time I checked."

My brother grimaces like I just told him all his money had been stolen. "Women get to decide what we men chose for them. You never seemed to understand that."

He's such a caveman. Honestly, I don't know how that girlfriend of his puts up with this kind of nonsense. He's probably completely pussy-whipped in private. That would be the only way any woman would tolerate this shit from him.

I don't bother trying not to roll my eyes. "Whatever, Matteo. So why am I here enjoying these luxurious accommodations?"

My snarkiness upsets him, and he takes a step

toward me like he plans to slap my face. I flinch, instantly hating that he sees he can have an effect on me like that.

Chuckling, he says, "You're here because it's time you settled down. I have the perfect husband for you, and it's going to be a beautiful wedding. Just like the one our father always looked forward to for you."

His words make no sense. Wedding? I'm not marrying anyone, particularly no one this shithead has chosen to be my husband. He's clearly lost his mind if he thinks this is actually going to happen.

"Matteo, I think you've been out in the sun too long. I'm not getting married," I say as calmly as I can, even while my heart races in utter terror.

He leans down so our faces are at the same level and smiles, but there's no happiness in his expression. "Yes, you are. Two days from now, you and Lucius Angeloni will become husband and wife. This is happening, so make it easy on yourself, Sienna, and accept it.

Lucius Angeloni? That guy who came in here before and spewed all that good girl bullshit? I don't think so.

"I won't do it. Even here, you don't have the power to force me to marry him."

Matteo shrugs like my protests mean nothing to him. "It's hard to imagine you spent your entire life here and you don't know how things work. Of course, I have the power to force you to marry him. I'd prefer not to have to go that route since it will likely make the party Lucius is throwing for the two of you uglier than it has to be, but no matter if you choose to fight this or not, it's happening."

Tears well in my eyes at the thought of having to marry some odious friend of my brother's. "I won't do it!" I cry, unable to control my emotions. "You'll have to drag me to the altar kicking and screaming, and still I won't do it. These aren't medieval times, Matteo. You can't force me to marry someone I don't love."

He rolls his eyes at my mention of marrying for love. That concept is entirely foreign to him, as it was to my father. Marriage is a matter of convenience and power to the men in my family. I don't know who this Lucius really is, but if my brother insists on my marrying him, it's because it benefits him.

Because for damn sure my happiness plays no part in this equation.

"You will, and no matter of fighting it will change that. Lucius is a wealthy man, but let me warn you. He's not a patient one, so you better stop with all this crying. He has no time for some sobbing little thing who can't see the way life must be. Consider yourself lucky, Sienna. Until Lucius and I struck our deal, I was going to have you killed for what you did to this family. Now we both benefit."

My tears roll down my face, making him appear like some blurry monster in front of me. I hate him with every fiber of my being. With every cell in my body. With every thought in my head.

And if he thinks he's going to marry me off to this

Lucius jackass or anyone else, he's sadly mistaken. I might be emotional right now, but I'll find a way to escape before I have to say I do.

"Now sit tight because the fun is just getting started."

He turns to leave me alone again in that dark room, like he's done me some favor and now I should reflect on how generous he's been with me. Well, fuck him.

As the door closes, I swallow my anger to save it for another time. For now, I just have to believe Alaric knows I've been taken and he's going to find me.

If not, then God only knows how I'm going to find my way out of this nightmare. But I will. Nobody is going to force me into marrying a man I don't love.

CHAPTER EIGHT

ucius

CIGAR SMOKE DRIFTS OUT FROM BETWEEN MY LIPS, and I tilt my head back to watch it float up into the air above me. Seated behind my desk in my office, I'm alone for the first time today and happy to have a chance to think about the woman who's set to become Mrs. Angeloni in less than forty-eight hours.

The memory of Sienna tied to that chair in the storage room at her brother's villa makes me smile. I always enjoy seeing a woman restrained. It never fails to make me hard as a rock. She better get used to that because I plan to tie her up often.

She best not get her hopes up that this is going to be some kind of love match, though. I've already got someone I enjoy. I don't need a wife to screw up that arrangement. The last thing I want is to have to deal with Maya getting all jealous.

Women. What a fucking hassle they can be.

No, Sienna is a means to an end. That idiot brother of hers is nowhere as intelligent as his father. Salvatore Rossetti was a man to be feared and respected because he understood how to handle the situations that come up when you have power.

Matteo, on the other hand, is like a greedy child. Always with his goddamned hand out demanding something. As if I, Lucius Angeloni, should be expected to simply give things away. He practically dumped that sister of his in my lap before I could finish telling him what I plan to give him for her.

Too fucking eager, he's so green when it comes to business. The problem is he needs money. I offered him land I own outside of Rome, but he almost begged me to sweeten the deal with cash. So I tossed out a number I knew would make his idiot heart skip a beat.

Two million euros. As if I'd pay that much for any woman, much less the far too Americanized Sienna Rossetti. Who wants a female whose head is full of all that bullshit from the States? No, thank you.

But I don't plan on having to keep her for long. Just long enough to secure my hold over Matteo and his family. Then I'll kill her and the rest of those fucking Rossettis and finally pay their father back for taking something that was mine all those years ago.

Salvatore may have forgotten our past, but I never did. I had hoped to exact my revenge on the man himself, but someone else got to him before I could. A pity, really. The bullet to his brain that assassin gave him was nothing compared to the suffering I had planned for him.

All water under the bridge, as they say. I don't really give a damn what member of that family bears the brunt of my revenge. One Rossetti is as bad as the next, so fuck it. I'll play with Salvatore's daughter for a little while, and then one by one, I'll get rid of each and every one of them.

And then I'll be left with all the wealth that never should have gone to that family in the first place. Revenge is a dish best served cold, and I'd say thirty years makes mine practically icy.

My eyes closed, I don't see my righthand man Antonio come into my office. He tears me out of my daydream about how satisfying it's going to be to finally give Matteo and the rest of them what they have coming.

"Lucius, the caterer wants to know if we want him to set up on the terrace or keep everything inside. He's worried about the weather tonight."

I open my eyes and exhale a deep sigh. Killing people is so easy. One or two shots and they're done. It's the rest of my existence as Lucius Angeloni that's taxing. As one of the wealthiest men on the Amalfi Coast, I'm expected to give lavish parties to impress upon everyone in this region how powerful I am, but damnit, they're a hassle. Caterers with their weather concerns. Chefs insisting on their favorite dishes instead of what I want. Decorators who demand to show off their creative talent and style instead of simply making my villa look impressive.

It's enough to make a man take out his gun and start shooting. Luckily for all the help I've hired, I'm a patient man. I swear, though, one of these days one of them is going to say the wrong thing and they're going to vanish from the world.

Antonio stands a few feet in front of my desk waiting for my response, his hands stuffed into his front pockets and his shoulders hunched, as if dealing with all of this nonsense leading up to tonight's party is wearing him down. I know how he feels.

"Cheer up," I say as I run my hands through my hair. "You look like you're going to collapse under the weight of something heavy."

That makes him smile, and he takes a step toward me as he says, "I honestly don't know how you do it. You give eight, maybe nine parties a year, and I swear it's the same goddamned hassles every time. I told the caterer I'd check with you about where to set up, but I really wanted to just chuck him over the side of the terrace and watch him tumble down the hillside."

The palpable frustration in Antonio's voice reminds me of how I used to feel when I had to deal with all these people. Not that I don't have to manage everything, even though I have him to listen to them. Instead of just one of us getting annoyed, now we both get pissed off.

I laugh at the thought of that pain in the ass

caterer bouncing down the hill, but as much as the idea amuses me, I need him to make sure tonight goes as planned. Still, maybe after the party is over I'll let Antonio take out his aggravations on him.

"The weather will be fine, but let him set up everything inside. That way if his worries about rain come to pass, we'll be covered. Not that I expect some kind of torrential downpour that will soak the terrace. I can't remember the last time that happened. He's just being overly cautious."

Antonio twists his expression into a deep grimace and rolls his eyes. "He's just a pain in the ass. I'll tell him what you want, though. Do you have any other message for him?"

My mind flashes the memory of all those men in black tuxes the caterer mistakenly used a few parties back. Jesus Christ. Who wants to see a room full of men walking around with trays at a party? I threatened the poor bastard's life after that.

"Remind him that if I see male waiters at this party that he won't work in this region again. I want to see women wearing practically nothing walking around showing off the goods for my guests. The people I invite to my home don't come here for a room full of fully dressed dicks. They want skin and good-looking skin at that. Make sure he knows that, so we don't have another screw up like we did a few months ago."

The mention of beautiful women wearing next to nothing makes Antonio's mood perk up. With a smile, he says, "I'll be sure to tell him that. The last thing anyone wants is a goddamned sausage fest here tonight."

I shake my head at his descriptive way of describing a room full of men in tuxes. That year he spent working for my brother in New York left him with some odd behaviors, and the way he refers to things is definitely one of them.

"Sausage fest. Some of the things you say make me laugh."

He begins to explain the reason he used that term, but I wave him away, uninterested in its background. It's an apt term. It's just so American that it hits my ears oddly.

Left alone to devise my plans for the night, I wait for Matteo to show up for our meeting. He knows what I'm going to demand from him, but I still want to make sure I'm in the right frame of mind for when he gets here.

Don't let anyone ever try to tell you it's not exhausting pretending to be someone you're not. Every moment I have to spend with that man drains my energy. I just keep telling myself I've waited this long to get back at the Rossettis, so a few more hours of playacting like I'm happy to be conducting business with him won't be bad.

Ten minutes later, a knock on my office door alerts me to his arrival. Straightening myself in my chair, I call out for him to come in. It's nearly showtime.

Matteo Rossetti walks into the room like he's entitled to everything I have, instantly annoying me. I cannot let this upset me. I push my true feelings down inside and force a smile onto my face as I stand up to greet him.

"Matteo, good to see you. Are you ready for a night you'll never forget?" I ask as we shake hands.

Not that he'll be able to remember anything once he's dead and gone from this world.

"My brothers and I are looking forward to tonight," he says with a smarmy smile as he sits down in front of my desk.

"And your sister? Is she too looking forward to my party tonight?"

His smile fades away. "I haven't mentioned anything about it to her yet. I saw no need to excite her any more than I already have. Sienna can be a handful when she's upset."

He instantly realizes what he's said and quickly adds, "But you won't have to worry. She'll be as accommodating as you want her to be. Trust me. She's just a bit difficult with me because I'm her brother."

Since everyone around here knows how I handle women, his attempt to lessen my concerns about his feisty sister are unnecessary. She'll do as I want, or she'll feel the sting of my hand on her skin.

"Well, I look forward to seeing her and your entire family here tonight. They will all be here, won't they?"

I have to curb my enthusiasm, or he may suspect something is wrong about the party tonight. Then again, Matteo Rossetti isn't very smart, so he might not pick up on anything.

He nods quickly, as if he's eager for me to know he's bringing the whole clan to my party. I don't think he even knows this about himself, but he's very much the pleaser. His father probably made him like that. Or it could be the money he thinks he's getting from me in return for that sister of his in fueling his enthusiasm.

Whatever the reason, I appreciate him behaving like he needs to make me happy.

Turning in my chair, I reach over to the crystal decanter of scotch nearby on the bar and grab it along with two glasses. "Let's toast to the joining of our two families."

"Yes, let's! It's going to be a fine day when the Rossetti and Angeloni families merge," Matteo says enthusiastically.

I smile at him, enjoying how eager he is. This is almost too easy.

I pour the two of us our drinks and slowly push his toward the edge of my desk. He grabs it before it falls off and raises his glass into the air.

"To the merger that will change the Amalfi Coast for good!" he says with far too much cockiness.

For good, indeed. That's downright laughable, but he has no idea of what's in store for him.

"To the merger!" I respond before taking a gulp of my drink.

Setting my glass down in front of me, I say, "I expect her to be dressed in something far more appropriate than the rags I saw her in the other day.

She needs to look like she belongs in the Angeloni family."

Matteo doesn't sense the change in my tone or my subtle dig at his family. Instead, he nods his head again and smiles, happy to tell me what I want to hear.

"Not to worry. I can assure you I've taken care of everything. Sienna will be nothing short of the most beautiful woman here tonight. I've spared no expense."

I silently scoff at the thought that his sister could ever be the most beautiful woman in my home on any day. For God's sake, the women serving food to my guests will likely be more beautiful.

"Good. I'm happy to hear that. I look forward to showing her off to my guests, so knowing you've handled all the required details to make her look like she belongs here puts my mind at ease."

Matteo takes another sip of his drink and stands to leave. "I better get going. I have an entire family to handle today. I look forward to the party, Lucius. Tonight's been a long time coming."

I stand to shake his hand and smile at how prophetic his words are. "Indeed it has. Too long, but everything has a season. I'm happy we've finally reached this one."

His smile tells me he's unsure of my cryptic message, but no matter. He'll find out soon enough what it all means.

"Until tonight, Lucius," he says before turning around and walking out.

"Until tonight."

Antonio comes back into the office a few minutes later. "I saw Matteo Rossetti leave. He looked happy. I was a little surprised to see that."

I throw my head back in laughter. My righthand man so often tends to be too serious. "We can allow him a little happiness today considering what's in store for him. Let him smile. It will make what I have planned even more fantastic when he finally realizes he's fucked with the wrong man."

"It's been a long time coming, Lucius. I don't know how you've stayed so patient. I wouldn't have been able to be that calm."

I study Antonio for a long moment and decide he's telling the truth. He's far too combustible for revenge. He would have struck at Salvatore Rossetti two days after his betrayal. The idea of waiting years to get back at that family is something entirely foreign to him.

Not everyone can be as cold-hearted as I am. That's why I have all I want in the world, and he works for me.

"Time is almost up for Matteo and his family. The sins of the father will indeed be visited on the son and on all of Salvatore's children. I bet he died thinking I was one of his closest friends, as ridiculous as that sounds."

Antonio shakes his head and sighs. "You can't help stupid, I guess. The fact that he could even think you two were anything other than sworn enemies after what he did to you is unbelievable."

I shrug, happy to know my vengeance is coming soon now. "A man will believe what he wants to believe when he has the world by the tail. Unlike his father, though, Matteo Rossetti does not control this coast anymore. As soon as his father was found slumped over his desk, I knew my time had come. Patience is more than merely a virtue, my friend. It's an absolute necessity when you're dealing with villains."

He laughs because he knows I'm every bit as much the villain as those I hate. But there's one difference between all of them and me.

Patience.

CHAPTER NINE

laric

WHILE I ENJOY A MIDDAY DRINK AT THE HOTEL BAR, I listen for information about the party Gideon told me about earlier in the day. Lucius Angeloni plans to throw a big event tonight, no doubt to announce his intended wedding to Sienna, and I plan to be there.

I just don't know how yet.

The one good thing I have going for me is that no one here knows me. While Gideon and I clearly resemble one another, I'm a stranger here, for the most part. I plan on using that to my advantage to get to Sienna and take her away from this madness her brother set in motion.

At least I know she's safe. Her brother will want to keep her alive and well so he can marry her off. What conditions he's kept her in for the past few days while he's held her here are unclear as of yet. I can only hope that Matteo Rossetti honors something of the family ties he and his sister share.

I listen to the chatter at the tables around me as hotel guests talk about the Angeloni get-together and how he never fails to throw the best parties. Two men at a table directly behind me can't wait to enjoy the sights which include the gorgeous women he always has working as servers whenever they go to his home.

This guy sounds like some Italian version of Hugh Hefner, for fuck's sake. The more I listen to the men talk, the more I wonder if getting into his home tonight will be as dangerous as I initially thought.

Gideon sits down in front of me with a bottle of something clear and sets it down between us. Staring at me while I eavesdrop on the conversation at the next table, he looks like a combination of amused and irritated.

"Listening in on my guests?" he asks sharply, as if I'm doing something egregious that breaks some unwritten hotel rule.

I wave off his question as the men behind me talk about some time when they were at Angeloni's villa for a party and the entire thing turned into an orgy. Fucking Hefner wannabe.

Finally, the men laugh and get busy eating their meal, so I turn my attention to Gideon not so patiently waiting for me to finish my prying. "Do you ever just people watch here? You must get some very interesting people coming through this place."

"I'm a little busy for snooping on people's private conversations. This place doesn't run itself, as much as I wish it would," he says in a distinctly disapproving tone.

"I'm trying to find out all I can about this party tonight," I say in a hushed voice. "It's not really snooping if you're doing it for a good reason."

That makes him laugh, and with a wicked smile, he shakes his head. "So noble. Have you found out anything useful, or just the usual gossip about the host tonight?"

I look around, glancing back at the men behind me who now seem completely distracted by their cell phones, and then return my attention to my cousin. "The guy sounds like he's trying to create the Amalfi Coast version of the Playboy mansion. I heard the word orgy used at least twice."

Gideon rolls his eyes. "I guess if the Marquis de Sade was running the place, then maybe. I've been to a few of his parties. Always beautiful, half-naked women roaming around with trays of exquisite food and drink. That's not a bad thing, of course, but that's not what I'm ever there for myself."

Curious about his seemingly disdainful attitude toward what sounds like a good reason to attend a party in the first place, I ask, "If you're not there for beautiful women, then what are you there for?"

A wolfish smile lifts the corners of his mouth, and I

swear I see a sparkle in his eyes. "Information, of course. I may look like the man in charge of the Villa Aurelia, but my real job here, as I'm sure you know, is to be the eyes and ears of our family's business in Italy. Helix Rule can't be here, so that's where I come in."

I study my cousin for a long moment and shake my head. "You know what they say. All work and no play make Gideon a very dull boy."

"Don't worry about me. I get my fun when I want it. Tonight, though, won't be one of those times."

For the first time since he sat down, I straighten myself in my chair. "No, it won't be. We need to find Sienna and get her away from him before he and her brother do something that hurts her."

Gideon leans forward toward the middle of the table and whispers, "About that. From what I've been told, her brother has her holed up at the family estate. It's not the best accommodations and certainly not how I'd treat my sister, but she's okay. They haven't been beating her, for the most part, and she's unharmed, generally."

My hands curl into tight fists as I try to temper my anger at hearing Sienna's only generally unharmed. When I get my hands on Matteo Rossetti, the same won't be able to be said about him, that asshole.

"Great fucking family she's got there," I mumble.

My cousin leans back in his chair and looks up toward the crystal blue sky and bright midday sun. "Not one I'd want. How bad did you go off on my father and Uncle Nick for letting them get her?"

As close as Gideon and I are, I know whatever I say next will go directly back to my two uncles, so I weigh my words carefully as I decide how to answer. "It wasn't entirely their fault. They checked out the boyfriend, and he cleared. Her family must have gotten to him. Fucking Trent. I'll get him for this after I finish things here in Italy. Asshole."

Lowering his head, Gideon smiles. "Trent? He sounds like an asshole. I think I remember a Trent from school. If I'm thinking of the right person, Alex and he got into it more than once his last year."

I laugh at Gideon's statement, as if his brother so rarely fights. "Alex gets into it with everyone. I swear to God he's fueled by pure rage ninety percent of the time. Where's he get that? It's not like you or your parents are like him," I say.

With a shrug, my cousin answers, "I have no idea. We aren't exactly best friends. I think he might be a vampire with the way he spends all day in bed and only comes out at night."

Considering that Alex runs one of Helix's nightclubs, I guess it's normal that he prefers to sleep during the day. Not that I think anything about that cousin is normal. When he's not so full of anger that he's practically growling at people when he answers them, he's silent and surly and ignores anyone who dares to be around him.

"Well, he probably has to be a bit of a night owl to do what he does for a living, don't you think?" I ask.

Gideon simply shakes his head. "I guess. My older

brother and I don't seem to have a lot in common, so I can't honestly tell you why he is the way he is. Let's just say the way you two get along, or don't get along, is barely worse than the way we get on."

His brother reminds me of my older brother, and I say, "You know who he's most like in our family? Goddamned Sebastian. They've had every opportunity in the world, and still they walk around like their entire lives are fucking miserable."

"The curse of the firstborn?" Gideon asks with a chuckle.

"Doesn't sound like much of a curse to me. Ask your father if my father ever seemed cursed by being the firstborn and I think he'll tell you that's bullshit. They get everything they want. Can you say you've been that lucky?"

My cousin looks around the gorgeous terrace off his five-star hotel and then back at me. With a sly grin, he answers, "I'm not sure I'm a good person to ask. I get to live here and run this place. Not exactly a hardship, Alaric. Now you, I get your resentment toward your father and brother. Thank God you showed up at my father's doorstep. Our side of the family is more like you anyway."

I nod at that little bit of truth. "Absolutely. I can't imagine being stuck in Connecticut dealing with Maddox and Sebastian Rule. No, thanks. I'm all good with what Helix has me doing. Not that I'm on the job here now, of course. This is personal thing."

A stunning woman with long black hair wearing a

red dress that hugs every gorgeous inch of her voluptuous body strolls by the table, making both of us turn our heads to watch her as she walks over to a table of three other beautiful women. Gideon's right. This job certainly wouldn't qualify as a hardship, for sure.

When she sits down, the two of us look back at each other and smile. "I thought you were in love," Gideon says with a smile.

"I may be in love, but I'm not dead. I still have eyes that can see when a beautiful woman passes by me," I answer truthfully.

As if I said something that displeased him, he frowns and sighs. "Love. Hmmm. You'll have to let me know how that works out for you. I've never found it to be something worth my time."

With a chuckle, I say, "Maybe you should try kidnapping someone. It worked for Sienna and me. Maybe it could work for you too."

Gideon opens his mouth to say something but closes it almost immediately before finally saying, "Who knew kidnapping was the way to a woman's heart?"

I look around the terrace and in through the large doors leading into the hotel's restaurant. "And you have a great place to keep someone. I mean, what woman wouldn't want to stay here?"

Shaking his head, he answers, "I'm going to end this conversation since I don't have any idea what to say. As for the party tonight, I think I just saw someone who can get you an invitation to tonight's festivities so we don't have to have you scaling Angeloni's villa's walls like you're fucking Romeo."

I follow his gaze to a woman behind me who's just walked out onto the terrace from inside. Attractive with platinum blond hair and what looks to be a cool million in diamonds hanging around her neck, she appears a little older than the kind of women I assume Gideon prefers.

"Someone you know well? Or intimately?" I ask as he stands up from the table.

He looks down at me and gives me a knowing smile. "I've been known to sample the local delicacies from time to time. She's not one I've ever tried, though. Give me a few minutes."

I watch him walk over to her and see her smile broadly when he kisses her hand. Gideon knows how to schmooze with the best of them, and as the one who runs this hotel, I imagine he has contacts all over the coast. Good. I'd rather not pull my Romeo and Juliet routine trying to get into Angeloni's villa tonight. I can, but I'd rather reserve my efforts for when I have to get Sienna the hell out of there.

He and the woman disappear into the hotel, leaving me to try to enjoy this beautiful day while I wait for him to return with good news. I feel guilty reveling in the sunlight and surrounded by beautiful people while Sienna is being kept in God only knows where on the Rossetti estate. I'd bust up in there now if I thought I could find her and get her away from there, but I know better.

The last time I entered the family's villa to kill her father, they didn't know I was coming. The benefit of surprise helped immeasurably, as it always does. But this time Matteo likely believes he needs to keep a close eye on his sister since he's clearly planning on using her to better his fortunes with Angeloni.

I may not know everything about getting into this party, but the information I've gleaned about the man himself tells me all I need to know about this merger between those two families. Matteo's got power, but he needs money. Angeloni is a longtime friend of Salvatore Rossetti with loads of cash, but he wants some of the power of his expected in-laws. So Matteo gets a much-needed infusion of cash, and Lucius Angeloni gets a new plaything to amuse him on top of being connected through marriage to the mafia power in the region.

Everyone wins. Except Sienna, of course.

That's where I come in. Tonight, whether I get an invitation or not, I'm going to be at that party to rescue her. Her brother made a mistake taking the woman I love. I'll have to get over the guilt of not watching over her myself more closely, but Matteo Rossetti is the one who's going to pay for what he's done to her.

Lost in thought about all I'm going to do to exact my revenge on that son of a bitch brother of hers, I don't see Gideon sit down until he slides a gold envelope across the table toward me. I guess his friend there got me an invitation to tonight's party.

"There you go. I knew Giulia would find a way to help us out. All it cost me was a weekend in one of the best suites in the hotel, small change for what she gave me," Gideon says with an expression of pure satisfaction.

I stare at him for a moment wondering if she gave him something else to put that look on his face but decide not to ask. Maybe he didn't get a quick blowjob on top of the invitation. Maybe he just enjoys getting people to do what he wants when he asks for things.

But I can't stop myself from saying, "Any chance that weekend includes you? Because you look pretty damn pleased about something right now."

He shakes his head. "Never mind why I look pleased right now. Let's just say I like when things go smoothly with any part of my life and leave it at that. Now you can't go to this party as Alaric Rule. I don't want our names connected like that, so you need to figure out who you're going to be."

"Not interested in explaining who I am, Gideon? I think I might be insulted," I tease as I run my fingertips over the embossed lettering on the white invitation.

He grimaces at my joking. "I never like having to explain myself or what I'm up to. Better to have you be someone not related to me since I have to live here after you get to grab the runaway bride and ride off into the sunset."

"Fair enough. I've got other IDs I can use. Just tell me one thing. Am I going to understand a goddamned thing tonight since I don't speak Italian?"

That makes him throw his head back in laughter. "Such a typical American," he chides me. "Yes, you'll be able to understand people. Many of them speak English, so if you feel the need to talk to someone, you should be fine. If you need something translated, just find me. I speak the language fluently."

I don't know why hearing that surprises me. "Really? I had no idea."

"I live here, for Christ's sake, Alaric. I wouldn't be able to do my job if I couldn't speak the language of the locals. On top of that, I'd never hear anything about what goes on around here if I didn't speak Italian. It's just a matter of usefulness."

Gideon Rule, jack of all trades.

Holding the invitation up in front of me, I say, "Thank you for this. I'm sure Sienna will be happy to thank you too once I get her out of there. I owe you, Gideon."

He waves away any mention of being owed anything. "It was nothing. A quick ask, a giveaway of my best suite for a couple days, and voila! You're invited to the party of the year. Just don't expect it to be easy, Alaric. You may have been able to get into the Rossetti villa to kill her father two years ago, but Angeloni's estate is going to be heavily guarded. I've gotten you in. Now you need to figure out how you're going to get out with Sienna."

"And not get us both killed," I add with a chuckle.

With a serious look, Gideon leans toward me and whispers, "Laugh all you want, but I wasn't kidding when I said the place is going to be heavily guarded. Angeloni may not be the kingpin like Salvatore Rossetti was and what his son is trying to be after his father's death, but he's vicious. In fact, I'd probably rather go up against Matteo than Lucius Angeloni, if I had a choice."

"Don't worry about me. I'll take care of things. I always do, don't I?" I ask, confident in my ability to do my job like I always have.

Gideon thinks about my claim for a few seconds and then tilts his head left and right. "You do, but this is different, isn't it? You aren't usually riding in on your white horse and rescuing a damsel in distress."

I roll my eyes at that ridiculous description. "First of all, I don't ride horses, so let's get that straight. Second of all, you can trust me when I say Sienna Rossetti is a lot of things, but a damsel in distress isn't one of them. If I know her, she's been a royal pain in the ass the whole time she's been kept at her brother's house. I'd bet he's regretted bringing her back here more than once in the past few days. If it wasn't that he was going to benefit so handsomely from this merger of his family with Angeloni's, he probably would have cut her loose by now. Sienna is a handful. Trust me on that."

"All that aside, just keep your eyes open tonight. I'll be there to help with the Italian, but I can't go helping you stealing Angeloni's intended away from right under his eyes. Remember, I need to live here tomorrow."

I lift my drink and smile across the table at my favorite cousin. "Got it. Get in, get the girl, and get the hell out without ruining the Rule family name and all you've got going on here. Piece of cake."

He looks at me like he knows I'm being too cocky, but I've done harder jobs as this before. I just need to keep my emotions out of the job. I can do that.

I've always done it before.

CHAPTER TEN

ienna

I CAN'T BREATHE IN THIS RIDICULOUS GET-UP MY brother has me in tonight for this party. Not that it matters to him. My job is to look good. Breathing is optional, I guess.

Glancing down my body, I inwardly cringe at the silver dress hugging every inch of my curves. This is how I'm supposed to formally meet my future husband? Is he a pimp? Has my brother chosen to marry me off to a man who thinks women should parade around in tight dresses with slits up to their nether regions like I am tonight? One wrong move and everyone at this party, man or woman, is going to know me intimately.

When I lift my gaze to the room around me, I get

the answer to my question. Beautiful women with bodies I think must be full of silicone and definitely have been bought and paid for stroll around in tiny outfits more suited to nightclubs or the beach than the home of a man Lucius Angeloni's age and supposed standing in the community.

One woman smiles at me and gently pushes a silver tray of hors d'oeuvres toward me. "Would you like some? They're calamari," she says in a tiny voice that sounds like it belongs to a toddler and not a woman old enough to carry around enormous breasts that are barely being contained by the red fabric bikini top.

I cringe at the thought of trying to chew something rubbery at this moment. With a shake of my head, I beg off. "No, thank you."

Leaning in toward me, she whispers almost sadly in my ear, "Your dress is beautiful."

I force a smile and thank her before she strolls away to her next guest, now sure I must look like a hooker. Great. I used to live in this part of the world for a long time. There's a real possibility that I'll know someone here tonight. Imagine what they'll think of me like this.

"Oh, she thought she was so special going off to some elite school in America, but look at her now. She's nothing more than a made-up whore." I can hear the insults already.

If they only knew how much I don't want to be here dressed like anything tonight. I'm simply a pawn to be moved around my brother's chessboard, and tonight the square I get to stand on is here at the Angeloni villa.

My brother's men surround me like I'm a risk for flight. In this dress? They must be idiots. Likely, it's more that they're simply good soldiers obeying my brother's orders to keep me in their sights at all time.

None of these men have to worry. Where would I be able to go in this dress? Two steps and every guest here will see what only a few select men in my life have laid eyes on.

My mind drifts to the question of whether Alaric even knows I've been taken yet. It's been days. He must know, right?

But knowing and being able to save me from this nightmare are two very different stories.

From behind me, my brother leans in next to my left ear and whispers, "You better behave tonight, Sienna. There's a lot riding on how things go here with Lucius."

I spin my head to face him and snap, "Like my happiness? Is that what you're referring to, Matteo?"

As he has too many times since he dragged me back here, he grabs my upper arm and squeezes the flesh until tears fill my eyes. I cry out but his glare terrifies me, so I shut my mouth quickly.

"Good girl. You learn fast. I guess all that special schooling did do something for you after all."

I don't respond, even though I want to tell him to fuck off and that my time at Brown and Yale did not teach me how to act like he thinks a woman should. My brother is worse than a Cro-Magnon. He's an animal, pure and simple, and while college didn't teach me how to handle creatures like him, my common sense tells me not to arouse his anger more than I already have tonight, or he may do something truly terrible to me.

Well, more terrible than marrying me off to a man who had no qualms about seeing me tied up and held hostage in a chair for days.

He steps away from me, taking the two goons that were standing to my left with him, and I glance in that direction to see my reflection in the window across the room. Oh, God. This dress is so humiliating. Silver, as if that's ever looked good on anyone, it barely covers my breasts and the slit up the side goes straight up to my waist. His men took my clothes from me, including my underwear, and when Matteo presented this lovely gift to me, it didn't include any replacement panties.

So here I stand as still as a statue in the desperate hope that if I remain utterly immobile no on will see the goods. But I guess showing off my goods is exactly what the intent of this dress is. Subtlety doesn't seem to be a trait Matteo or Lucius possess.

God, my brother is a pig. So must this future husband of mine be if he thinks dressing his fiancée like this is anything good.

I scan the room I'm in and see money in the décor. The white marble pillars alone set Lucius back thousands, I'm sure. Expensive Persian rugs in this room and the one next to it scream money, as does the priceless Etruscan vase collection I saw displayed in special alcoves in the entryway.

So I'm to be given away to a wealthy older man. This is exactly why I wanted to get as far away as possible from my family. Twenty-two years old and forced to marry a man I don't love. For God's sake, I don't even know him, and what I do know I don't like. If he's friends with my brother, then he's no one I'd ever want.

Focused on the gold and crystal dotting the decorations around me, I don't realize someone's joined me and my remaining guards until he steps so close to me that his chest brushes against my breasts. I instantly recognize him from when I was being held at the house. He's the man who came in to talk to me that time. He's dressed in a black tux and looks more civilized, but he's the same person who joked that we'd have fun together.

My future husband, Lucius Angeloni, I presume.

He ogles me like I'm something he's considering buying to add to his collection of expensive looking things. I try not to meet his gaze as I study this person, but he seems intent on looking into my eyes, as if there's some secret in them he's eager to learn.

There's nothing you want behind these eyes, buddy. Just a brain, and why would you want a woman to have one of those?

His short, dark hair has enough gray in it that anyone can tell with a cursory glance that he's considerably older than me. He exudes something that comes off as power at first, but a hint in his expression tells me it's more cruelty than strength. No wonder my brother thinks so highly of him.

As I examine the man who's to be my husband, he lifts his hand and trails his forefinger along my jaw. With a smile, he says in a low voice, "I hope you're having a nice time here in my home tonight, Sienna."

I want to say this is the last place on earth I want to be tonight, but I know better, so I force myself to smile sweetly and reply, "Thank you for your generous hospitality. Your home is lovely."

More hollow words may never have come from my mouth, but he seems to enjoy them, if his broadening smile is any indication. Good to know. He responds to flattery. I'll definitely have to keep that in mind.

He steps closer to me, eliminating the tiny bit of space that existed between us, and says in a low voice, "I think these guards can go away, don't you?"

I don't sense he wants my opinion on this subject and instead would like my appreciation, so I open my eyes wide like his offer is the most wonderful thing I've ever heard and pretend to be thrilled he's about to give me some tiny measure of freedom. Not that I could do much with it, unless I want to flash his guests my girly bits on my way over to the bar.

Before I can mutter my thanks in a baby voice similar to the server's before, he adds, "I'm expecting you to behave yourself, Sienna. Don't disappoint me."

His unspoken warning is clear, and fear rushes

through me with each syllable he utters in my ear. Be good or get hurt. I'm a smart girl. I know how this works. I guess maybe I just thought he'd try something like charm on me before moving straight to threats.

Foolish me. But in truth, why would he try to be nice? He doesn't have to be. He's seen how my brother held me in that tiny room for days. Why should he do any better?

With a wave of his hand, my guards move away. My brother returns to my side not a minute later and instantly notices his men have been dismissed. Displeasure covers his expression, chilling me to the bone. Does he think I did something to make them go?

"Where are my men?" he asks me, as if I have the power to make them disappear.

Lucius answers for me. Turning his attention from his fascination with me, he looks at my brother sternly. "I sent them away. Sienna is to be treated as the woman of this house, not some criminal."

And just like that, my brother thinks my not being guarded is a fantastic idea. "Oh, yes. Of course. It's only right," he gushes, as if it was his idea in the first place.

He's not only a pig but an obsequious one.

For a moment, I breathe a tiny bit easier, but Lucius's voice in my ear sends any comfort I felt fleeing when he says, "I'll hurt you if you displease me, so don't make me unhappy. This is your first test, Sienna."

I wish I could make some snappy crack about being great at taking tests since I did so well in school, but I'm too afraid at this moment to try to sound brave. This man is far crueler than my brother, and I suspect he revels in hurting people even more than Matteo does.

So all I do is smile like his happiness is the only thing on my mind. Little does he know that even now I'm conjuring up ideas on how to find a way to get away from him. If that means he has to be hurt or worse, so be it. I might only be a woman in the Rossetti family, but I learned a few things from my father in his life. When the time comes for me to escape this marriage, I'll do whatever it takes to get away.

Including burying a knife in my dear husband's heart and watching blood spurt from his chest like a geyser as he lies dying in front of me. He and my brother have forgotten that Rossetti blood flows through my veins. I may have tried to forget that for many years, but now that I'm back here and being traded for God only knows what, all I learned growing up as the daughter of Salvatore Rossetti is coming back to me clear as day.

A patient, smart woman with a taste for vengeance isn't someone you want to fuck with, gentlemen. Remember that.

Lucius and Matteo walk away, leaving me truly alone for the first time tonight. Every cell in my body screams for me to make a break for it, but how? In this get-up, they'd catch me in under a minute, and then I'd be even worse off than I am right now.

So I stand in these four-inch heels Matteo forced me to wear and in this dress that makes me look like a cheap prostitute in a garish gown and gaze around the room at the guests that have come to Lucius Angeloni's home tonight. All dressed in tuxes and pricey designer gowns, the men and women smile and laugh as they enjoy their drinks and food handed out by the girls in bikinis. To them, this must be normal. To me, it seems utterly crass and ugly, but then again, I get to be the bought and paid for prize tonight.

My stomach roils at the thought of what's going to happen at the end of this night. The next few hours will be my last chance at freedom before I have to sleep with a man twice my age whose streak for nastiness is already far too obvious for this girl.

I feel like all eyes are on me, as if everyone here knows my fate at the conclusion of this party, and they see nothing wrong with that. No one appears to look at me like I'm someone in danger and in need of protection. No, if anything, all I see in their eyes is admiration when our gazes meet.

Or maybe that's just wishful thinking. They probably see me like I do right now. Like a paid for creature with no freedoms. How they could be okay with that I don't understand because I'm certainly not fine with any of this.

The question is how do I get the hell away from

this world I've been forced into first by my brother and now by Lucius?

Humiliation grows inside me until I feel my cheeks heat from a deep blush. I'm not just some piece of flesh to be traded from one man to another. It doesn't matter if anyone in this room knows that or even cares.

And then as if God has heard my silent pleas for help, I see the face of the one person who can get me away from this place. Near the entrance to the terrace, he stands with a glass of champagne in his hand looking as charming as all the other guests. Dressed in a tux, he looks more beautiful than I've ever seen him before.

Alaric.

Suddenly, I don't feel like all is lost. I don't know how he found me or what he's doing here dressed like that, but I know one thing deep in my marrow.

If he's here, I'm going to be safe.

If he's here, then he's got a plan. Now I just have to find a way to get to him so we can set it in motion.

CHAPTER ELEVEN

laric

I SEE HER THE MOMENT I STEP OUT ONTO THE terrace and instantly want to get her away from this place. She's dressed in something I know she had no part in choosing, evidenced by how uncomfortable she looks standing there.

She's as beautiful as always, though. No matter how her brother has tried to make her look, she's Sienna underneath that silver dress that shows off far too much for these people.

With a quick scan of the room, I see her brothers and any security intended to keep her in her place are on the other side of the room. They don't seem particularly interested in what she's doing either, which is good.

The man Gideon pointed out as Lucius Angeloni when we entered the villa appears busy with other guests and not the least bit interested in his intended wife. I suspect he assumes she's safe there alone since they're in his home, his turf where he controls everything.

Now is my chance to test that theory.

I give her a slight tilt of my head to let her know to come toward my side of the terrace and begin to casually walk over toward the railing overlooking the hillside. It's a beautiful, warm, late spring evening, and all I can think of is that I wish the two of us were anywhere else in the world together than this place.

But I can't focus on that now. Wishful thinking isn't going to get us the hell out of here and back to my suite at Gideon's hotel.

As I wait for her, I pretend to admire the view of the sea in the distance with the lights of the boats dancing off the water. It really is a gorgeous sight. I hope some night soon she and I will get to enjoy it from my balcony of my room.

Casually looking around for her, I see Sienna walking directly toward me. Her steps are awkward, and I let my gaze drift down her body to see she's wearing sky-high heels that make walking difficult, to say the least. She reminds me of a toddler taking her first steps.

When she gets close enough and I see there's no one near us, I whisper, "Don't face me. Look out toward the water like you're impressed."

She listens to me and does as I tell her to, even as I know she's desperate to get away from this place. "Alaric, please I need your help. My brother is planning to marry me off to Lucius Angeloni."

Rage courses through me like it's the first time I'm hearing that horrible idea. "When?" I ask through gritted teeth as I stare out mindlessly at the lights on the water.

"I don't know!" she says, her voice filled with terror. "He has me dressed up like some hooker and showing me off like I'm up for sale, but I'm here for that Lucius guy. He's the one who's the owner of this place. It might be tonight, for God's sake. It's not like they're interested in getting my permission or anything. Please, Alaric! I need your help."

Even as she whispers her answer, I hear the panic in her voice grow with each word. I need to let her know I'm here to take care of her.

"Don't worry. I'm here. I'll find a way to get you out."

But as I say that, I have to admit I'm not sure how quite yet. I'll figure it out, though. The woman I love needs me to save her, and that's what I intend to do.

"How? My brother has security to watch over me, and even though Lucius called them off, I'm sure he's got security too. We're surrounded here."

I want so much to turn to face her and take her in my arms as I tell her I know the odds are stacked against us, but I won't let her down. I wish she could see in my eyes how much I love her so she could know

I would never let her be married off to some guy in exchange for money her brother needs.

For now, though, we have to pretend like we're perfect strangers, each standing on the edge of this terrace staring out at the beautiful view in front of us.

"I promise I'll figure a way out of this," I whisper into the warm night air.

The sound of footsteps behind us reminds me that we're not alone. I turn to see Gideon leisurely strolling over toward where we stand. He stops on my right and looks out at the scene on the water with two boats flashing their lights as they pass one another, like an unspoken signal.

"Beautiful night, don't you think?" my cousin asks as if we're perfect strangers.

I feel Sienna's gaze on the side of my face as I nod like I want to be polite. "It is," I say, adding nothing to our conversation.

Sienna's confusion about how we're acting radiates from her, and I worry she might begin to start asking questions, so I glance around to see if there's anyone nearby and then whisper, "No one can know we're related. We're just three people standing here."

Her voice sad, she adds to the end of my statement, "At the top of a very large hill wondering if this is the only way out."

Gideon answers her whispered, desperate question. "It's not. We just have to be careful for the time being."

That does little to help ease either of our minds, if the way Sienna's tapping her fingers off the railing is any clue as to how nervous she is. Impatient, even though I know that's the worst thing I can be at this moment, I take a deep breath in to calm myself.

I've gotten out of more heavily guarded places than this before. Hell, I've gotten into more secure homes than this in the past.

The only difference this time is I won't be alone when I walk out of here. I have Sienna to think of, and dressed the way she is tonight, I doubt she'll be up for scaling any villa walls or jumping from windows.

No matter. I'll get her out of here.

"So what do we know about the security deeper in the house? I saw six guys around the front of the villa. What did you see as you walked through the rest of the villa, Gideon?"

Pretending to be someone who doesn't know me, he looks out at the water for a long moment and then runs his hands through his dark hair. "Not as many as you'd think, oddly enough. I suspect the owner thinks keeping people out is his main issue."

"Interesting. Okay. So the inside won't be the problem. Good." Turning my head ever so slightly in Sienna's direction, I ask, "Am I right in saying that your brother has four guards on you?"

She hums her answer and then adds, "But don't forget I have three other brothers here tonight too."

Each word sounds more frantic than the previous

one as she reminds me that Matteo Rossetti isn't the only family member willing to sell her off to Lucius Angeloni. Nice fucking relatives. I'm not even sure the Rules would do that to one of our own women.

"Good point. Gideon, anything we should know about the guests here tonight?"

My cousin shakes his head slowly. "Not that I know of, but I can't say I know each one of them."

"Fair enough. Why don't you wander around and scope out what's going on in the rest of the house? Look for any place to escape. Since you're known around here, Angeloni might not care as much as if I was checking things out."

He turns to leave and stops next to me to say, "Fine, but don't stay too long here with her. She's the center of attention and standing here with you is going to be more than obvious in only a few more seconds."

When he's gone and it's just Sienna and me again, I glance over at her and see her staring straight ahead with tears in her eyes and her hands clutching the railing in front of us. She looks so frightened that I can't decide if it's anger I'm feeling or sadness.

I can't afford to harbor any emotions tonight, though. Those I'll have to save for once she's safe and we're alone in my hotel suite. For now, I need to focus on the job at hand.

"What am I going to do if he takes me to his room?" she asks, her voice trembling. "You have to get me away from here before that happens because if you don't, he's going to—"

She doesn't finish her sentence, and I can't bear to think of what she's suggesting. "I will. Stay calm. You're strong. Remember the time you were kidnapped and made the guy fall in love with you?"

Out of the corner of my eye, I see her smile for the first time. It's a tiny grin, but it lights up her face. "Don't make jokes. I'm a woman in peril here, for God's sake."

We both turn to look at one another and I give her a smile. "I'd stack you in peril up against most people, never mind women, in this world, so just remember that. I need to go figure out the weakest security points inside this house, so stay out here as long as you can. Pretend to love the look of the water at night. Act like it makes you realize how much you miss being here in Italy. Anything that will discourage him from wanting to move you inside, okay?"

Her smile fades, and I see sadness fill her eyes. "Okay. You have no idea how happy I am that you found me, Alaric. I was worried you wouldn't, and I didn't know what I was going to do."

"I'll always find you, Sienna. Just like that day with your father's hitman. I'll always find you."

I hear her let out a heavy sigh, and then she whispers, "Thank you."

As I turn to walk back inside the house, I brush my arm against hers and whisper, "It's the least I can do for the woman I love."

She gives me a tiny smile I know she wishes could

be bigger. We'll have time for more smiles and happiness soon.

Right now, though, I need to prepare for the fact that tonight might get violent, and my only concern is making sure Sienna isn't hurt. As for the bastards who thought they could take her and force her to marry Lucius Angeloni, I can't wait to make them pay.

CHAPTER TWELVE

ucius

THE MEN I TRUST MOST IN MY LIFE GATHER AROUND me in my study for drinks and to hear my announcement the rest of the party will be told later on tonight. These five men have been with me through thick and thin, through the best times and the worst times, especially during that point in my life when Salvatore Rossetti betrayed me like no other person in this world has ever dared to do.

Tonight, I pay him back for that. I only wish he was still alive to have to suffer through the news. Of all the men on the coast, Rossetti knew me better than anyone, including my penchant for violence. Once, he appreciated it for how valuable it was to him, but when he found it inconvenient, he made the bad choice to betray me for less than I'm paying for his daughter.

Not that I'm worried about the money. Once Sienna's my wife, it will only be a matter of disposing of her and her idiot brothers so I'm the sole owner of all things Rossetti. The villa. The wealth. The power.

And then my revenge will be complete.

I've waited a long time for this to happen. Even as patient as I am, I sometimes lay awake nights wondering it this day would ever come. But come it has, and I plan to revel in every delicious moment of it as I take Salvatore's only daughter to my bed and do as I choose to her.

"Lucius, who's the woman in the silver dress?" Tommaso Andrioli, one of my oldest and dearest friends, asks as Antonio pours them all a drink.

With a grin, I answer, "Sienna Rossetti, fresh from being in America for the past four years."

My righthand man gives me a sideways glance at my mention of her having been away at school in the States for all that time. He's concerned she won't be as easy to break as Italian women now that she's tasted all that freedom American women possess.

Antonio should know me better. There's never been a woman I couldn't bend to my will. Sienna Rossetti will not be the first either.

The men around me nod and hum as they take in the information I know makes them remember what her father did to me all those years ago. None of them say a word about it. They fear sending me into a rage as even the mere mention of Salvatore's treachery often has in the past.

I'm flush with success tonight now that the time has finally come for me to exact my vengeance on that entire family, so there will be no explosion of my temper this evening. Tonight is to celebrate my triumph over a longtime enemy.

"So what's the news you called us in here to share?" Basilio Connigliaro asks before taking a sip of his drink.

Always so impatient that one.

I lift my glass into the air and smile as I announce, "I'm marrying again, gentlemen. That woman out there, Sienna Rossetti, is going to be the next Mrs. Angeloni. The events of the past have finally come full circle."

Each man looks utterly impressed by my news, and they all raise their glasses in the air to toast my good fortune. They all know every last detail of how her father took something most valuable from me and how I planned to avenge that wrong someday. Well, that day has come, finally. The house of Angeloni will finally be on top again.

"After all this time, Lucius. Too bad her father isn't here to have to suffer through the ceremony," Tommaso says with a chuckle. "He forgot about the insult he gave you and your entire family all those years ago. I know it. If only we could see his face now."

My dear friend knows how true those words are.

Salvatore's memory about taking the woman I loved more than life itself faded over time. Likely, he never considered it to be a problem since I never let on how much that wound hurt me. I kept a smile on my face, kissed his cheek as if we were as close as ever, and hugged him to my breast as if the loss he inflicted upon me didn't harm me at all.

At first, I planned on simply pretending to be okay until I could return the favor to him someday, but as time passed, that thought evolved into something darker and more vindictive. It wouldn't be enough to merely steal a woman from him like he had from me. When I took something he loved, it needed to be more than just some mistress or even a wife.

It needed to be the only daughter he had.

So I waited while she grew up, never failing to notice how she matured each year. I thought it might be possible that my chance slipped through my fingers when he allowed her to go to America for school, but Salvatore's sloppy use of his power in this region sealed her fate. Forced to remain in Italy, she would be mine by the end of that summer home.

Until her idiot brother Matteo nearly ruined my entire plan by going behind his father's back to get rid of her. What a fool Salvatore's oldest son is! As if any woman would be worth a hitman's bullet. There are far easier ways to dispose of a sister than killing her.

Such as selling her off to the man who's waited decades to get his revenge through her.

"She's beautiful, isn't she?" Antonio asks the men in the room. "She'll make a perfect wife for Lucius."

All the men agree, and Basilio licks his lips before saying, "I'd say so. Young, fresh, and ready to learn some life lessons I doubt she's even considered yet, even at that fine school she attended."

His round face grows red as he talks about Sienna like that. A decent man would be offended by his friends discussing his future wife like that, but I have no interest in stopping them. Not only am I not decent, but this isn't a love match, and I have no intention of pretending it is.

This is revenge through the use of a young woman's body. Nothing more. She'll learn to endure what I force upon her, or she'll be broken by the experience. But she will obey me, and I will exact my vengeance on her.

"How did Maya take the news?" Antonio asks as he settles in with his own drink now that he's finished serving the rest of the group.

I shrug at the memory of her momentary unhappiness when I told her the other night. "She knows how this works. She can't be my wife, so she's either happy being my mistress or she can be out on the street. I give her that choice every time I marry, and she makes the same one every time. She's smart. She knows she won't find anything better."

Tommaso laughs at my truthful answer about Maya and points at me. "This will be how many wives now, Lucius? I've lost count."

"Four. If Alesia had been stronger, she would have been number four, but it's all for the best, I think, since Sienna is the prize I've been waiting for," I say with pride now that my revenge is almost complete.

"And what happened with her? One day she was here hosting parties as an intended wife should, and the next day she was creating a scene that one night and she was gone," he says, clearly angling to find out if I got rid of my last intended bride in the most complete sense.

I stare him down for a moment for being so impudent and asking about what I do with my women, but I can't condemn him for being curious. Each of these men is saddled with the same wife they've had for ages. They need something to amuse them.

"She wasn't strong enough to be the woman of this house. When I found that out, I let her go."

Antonio lifts his glass and adds, "Not until you gave her a little dose of your particular brand of punishment, though, boss. I bet she's still smarting from that beating."

I nod, remembering how enraged I was after her behavior that night that sent me into a blinding rage. "And now she knows what happens when she doesn't behave. I bet her next man will appreciate how I beat the brazenness out of her. I did him and all men a favor."

"So what about this new one?" Gabriel Montero asks, nudging Basilio next to him so they both chuckle at the question. "Is she going to be strong enough?

She's delicious, to be sure. One look at her in that dress tells anyone with a working pair of eyes that, but does she have what it takes to handle you?"

The room erupts into laughter at the mere possibility that any woman has what it takes to handle me. I'm Lucius Angeloni. No one handles me. Not man or woman, and especially not some young girl.

"This one has fire inside her," I say before taking a mouthful of my drink and letting it slowly slide down my throat, warming my insides as it makes its way to my bloodstream.

Gabriel's eyebrows shoot up into his forehead. "Do you really want that? Fire sounds like work."

"Let's just say I'm going to enjoy taking out my revenge on her and extinguishing that fire of hers at the same time. Then she might become a woman I want. Until then, she'll be what I want in between the sheets."

"Tell me, Lucius," Basilio says. "Did you dress her like that for your guests tonight? If so, you're an even better host than I thought."

I shake my head at the vision of Sienna out on my terrace standing as still as a statue in that gawdy silver dress her brother forced her to wear. The women serving the food and drink to my guests need to show skin. They're help, for fuck's sake. Sienna is the woman I'm about to announce as my intended wife, and he dresses her like some cheap whore.

I'm going to enjoy when I kill him. I truly am.

Leaning back in my chair, I shrug at how

ridiculous the entire situation is. "Did you get to see anything you like?"

Each man nods, clearly happy to get a peek at my new bride. Tommaso raises his hand and says, "All it took was a few steps and I got to see enough to make me like her."

"Then maybe I'll let you take a try of her before I marry her. After tonight, of course. This night is for me. Afterward, though? Who knows?"

My marriage to Sienna Rossetti isn't a romance. It's payback, pure and simple, so why shouldn't I let my best friends enjoy her if they so choose? What do I care? I plan to kill her and her entire family anyway, so they might as well get off on her while they can.

CHAPTER THIRTEEN

laric

As I walk through the garden outside of Lucius Angeloni's home, I feverishly try to think of a way to get Sienna out of this house. I can't let her be with him. I can't let her brother get away with marrying her off to this man. She's mine. And if it takes having to kill every single one of these people to get her free, then that's what I'll do.

I tilt my head back to look up at the stars and wish the two of us were back at that apartment of hers less than a mile away from school.

I was so sure that if I stayed away from her that she'd be safe. I wouldn't bring her into my world of death and murder and hit men, and in turn, she'd be happy.

I should have stayed away, but the other night I couldn't do it anymore. Two years without feel her lips on mine and her graduation meant I needed to see her. She deserved to get a gift from me.

Fucking Trent. I knew as soon as I saw that son of a bitch that he was no good. I don't care if Helix and Nick checked him out. I knew he was rotten. Turns out I was right.

Her brother got to him. Son of a bitch. When this is all over, I'll get that bastard back for doing this to Sienna.

But I can't focus on that right now, though. I need to figure out how to escape this place, and I need to find a way to get Sienna out of here safely.

I look around at the manicured gardens surrounding me. Lucius Angeloni has more than enough money to spend on statues and fountains and landscapers to create the most exquisite Italian garden. Why he fucking needs to have Sienna as his wife I don't understand.

There must be at least half a dozen women inside who I heard in passing tonight say that they would kill to be in her position. Why not take one of them as his bride?

Not that this marriage is anything close to real. He doesn't even care about her. So what's the point? Is this just a family thing? Is it merely the joining of the Rossetti and Angeloni families? It must be. Not that any of that means damn thing to me. I'm going to get her out of here, and she's going to be able to forget all about Matteo and Lucius.

And then it will just be the two of us. Maybe we can find a place together.

As soon as the thought enters my brain, I'm struck at how unique that idea is for me. I have never even once with any woman thought that I could make a life with them.

I think I could with Sienna, though.

Maybe I wouldn't be a hit man anymore. Maybe I would find something else to do. Maybe it's time. This is a young man's game. It could be time for me to get out while I'm still alive. I could get a regular job. I'm sure Helix has some position in his organization I can do.

We could live on the island with Helix and Kerry. That might be nice. I think Sienna would like the island, but if not, we could go somewhere else. I have money. The entire world is open to us.

I just need to get her away from here.

Footsteps tear me out of my thoughts, and I turn around expecting to see Gideon, who is supposed to be helping me find a way out of here. Instead, I see a different familiar face, someone who's been absent from my life for at least a year, maybe two since he looks older.

He looks more vicious than the last time I saw him too. Alexei Wolfe.

The question is what the hell is he doing here at

the Angeloni villa and at a party where Sienna is being announced as Lucius Angeloni's next wife?

Alexei spies me from across the garden. Slowly, he approaches me with a wicked smile so typical of him. He does enjoy being an unrepentant villain.

"What are you doing here, Alaric?" he asks as he stops a few feet away from me.

"I could ask the same thing of you. In fact, I was just about to. What the hell are you doing here, Alexei?"

His smile fades, and I notice it no longer goes all the way up to his eyes. Something looks wrong with him. It isn't just that it looks older. Now he looks like something's changed with him.

"I thought since I didn't see you for a year or so that you got out of the game," I say with a low chuckle.

Wolfe shakes his head slowly left and then right. "I thought about it. I scaled back what jobs I was taking. My wife would prefer if I would stay home more lately. But tonight, I had a reason to come here to see Lucius."

Now my curiosity is piqued. I study him for a moment wondering what on earth he could want with Angeloni tonight of all nights.

"So, what's your business here? You here on a job?"

Alexei frowns and gives me a single nod. "A job. Yeah, I guess you'd call it that, except it's more personal than professional."

His words are cryptic, and I'm not sure what he's talking about. So I wait for him to continue and when he does, I realize it is far more personal for him tonight.

He swallows hard and says, "My daughter was with this son of a bitch."

Fuck. Alexei's daughter was with Lucius Angeloni? Was she one of the women Gideon told me about who didn't make it out alive?

"You know about him? He likes to beat the hell out of women," Alexei says through gritted teeth.

I nod my understanding. "Yeah. He's a real fuck, especially to women. I'm sorry your daughter got wrapped up with him."

"Yes, and this time he picked on the wrong woman. He beat the hell out of her. She may never be the same again. Her mother and I have her back home now. She's safe, but every day that goes by, I can't stand to see how broken she is. So tonight, Angeloni gets a dose of his own medicine."

"Angeloni has a new woman," I say as bile rises up in my throat at that description. Sienna isn't his. I'll die before I let that happen.

"God help her," Alexei says in a serious voice. "He's the devil, Alaric."

"The woman he's supposed to marry is the woman I love," I say as I glance around us to make sure we're alone. "Her brother brought her here. Basically sold her off to Angeloni."

"So that's why you're here?"

135

"I'm not going to let him have her. She will be leaving this place with me tonight."

Alexei nods. "I don't want to step on any professional toes, but you don't need to do anything here, Alaric. This is my job. This is my play. Angeloni is mine for what he did to my daughter."

I think about how hard it must be for Alexei to admit that his child has been brutalized by this man. Instantly, I know I don't want to take this from him.

It would be the same thing as if someone had wanted to take my killing Sienna's father away from me.

"I won't get in your way, Alexei. I just need to get Sienna out. Whatever the hell you want to do to Lucius Angeloni, fucking do it. He's a bastard. Feel free to take out all the Rossettis too for doing this to Sienna."

Alexei smiles and lets out a chuckle. "I'll leave her family to you. Angeloni is mine, though. For every time he hit my daughter, for every bruise he left on her body. For every night that she can't sleep because she can't forget what he did to her, that's why that son of a bitch is mine."

"What's your plan? He's got a house full of people in there and guards all over the place. What are you going to do to get to him?" I ask, genuinely unsure any hitman can break through this asshole's security.

Alexei tilts his head left and right, cracking his neck. "I'm going to do what I always do. You know how it is with people like us. Your job getting someone out of this place is going to be much harder. Security is everywhere, but getting in was no problem."

"I scored an invitation as easily as I'm sure you did," he explains. "This fuck has no problem letting people into his home because he needs everyone to see how wealthy and prosperous and wonderful his life is. So getting in wasn't an issue, and I won't have a problem finding him alone either," Alexei says confidently.

Listening to him, I get the sense it wouldn't matter what obstacles were put in his way on this job. Angeloni fucked with Alexei's family. He'll do anything to get his revenge for that. I understand all too well what he's feeling.

"I do wish you well getting her out, though. Get her as far away as you can from this place, Alaric."

I look around the garden to check that we're alone and take a step closer to Alexei. "I will fucking gun down every single one of these people if it means that's what I have to do to get Sienna out. She's my only concern."

A slow smile spreads across Alexei's face. "Spoken like a man in love. Last time we ran into one another, you didn't look like a man willing to settle down then. Something's changed."

I look up toward the villa behind us, knowing the woman I love is in there. "What changed is I met Sienna. You know how it is. You're married."

Alexei shrugs and gives me a nod. "I do. I knew the minute I met Natalie that there would only be her for the rest of my life. If you found that, you're a lucky man, Alaric. Men like us don't often get that chance at happiness. Just don't make the mistake I made. Don't think that because you found happiness with her that your life is made. I thought that and then my daughter met this son of a bitch. Never let your guard down. Even if you turn your back on our world, the people we've dealt with all during our careers are still out there."

He turns to walk away, leaving me standing alone in the garden next to a statue of what looks to be Neptune or Poseidon. "I hope your daughter is going to be better sometime soon."

Alexei glances back and nods. "Thank you. I know I'll be better when this fucker's heart stops beating."

"Good luck, Alexei."

With a laugh, he moves away and says, "I don't need luck. You know how this works, but good luck with Sienna. Be careful getting out. But once you get her out, don't look back. Don't ever look back."

CHAPTER FOURTEEN

ienna

I FEEL SOMEONE COME UP BEHIND ME AND TURN around hoping to see Alaric there. But he's nowhere to be found, and instead it's Matteo glaring down at me.

"What are you doing over here? You're supposed to be the focal point of this party since your intended husband is going to announce your engagement tonight, and you're standing out here staring out at the fucking water like some lost child."

God, I don't think I could hate someone more than I do this person right now. Does he not get his payment from Lucius Angeloni if I take a few minutes to look out at the boats on the goddamned water?

I don't bother asking that question because the less

I have to deal with my brother the better. "What can I do for you, dear brother?"

My less-than-subtle snideness doesn't make him happy, and his frown deepens. "You cannot ruin all my plans simply because you don't want to accept what your responsibilities to our family are."

Such a tool.

Rolling his eyes, Matteo shakes his head in frustration with me, as ridiculous as that is. "I swear our father spoiled you, and now I have to deal with the fallout from his mistakes. He should have never let you go to America for school. That's where you got all these silly ideas in your head."

As much as I know I shouldn't take the bait, I can't help myself and blurt out, "Ideas like believing I should have the choice to marry or not and who I might want to actually spend my life with? Heavens, Matteo. You act as if I wouldn't have had those ideas if I stayed here in Italy. Your world here may still exist in the Middle Ages, but it's the twenty-first century for the rest of us. As for our father, considering what he tried to do to me, I don't think he's a good person to credit for my loving freedom."

My comment about our father makes my brother laugh, although I don't understand what the hell would be considered funny about a man wanting his only daughter killed. It's like the men in my family live in an alternate universe where women are nothing more than pawns to be moved around their chess boards, and when they no longer have any use, they're thrown away permanently.

"Father was always too fond of you, if you ask me. Now let's go find your fiancé and see what he wants you to do. It certainly won't be standing out here ignoring his guests."

Matteo wraps his meaty hand around my upper arm, squeezing my bicep until I cry out. Immediately, he leans down in my face and snaps, "Not another sound out of you, Sienna, or I swear to God I won't have a problem handing you over to Lucius with bruises all over your body. Now let's go!"

My brother drags me through the house and past guests who don't even blink an eye to a hallway. It's dark and ominous, like a precursor to what I'm about to experience with his buddy Lucius.

"Matteo, you don't have to do this," I say, my voice verging on begging him to stop before it's too late.

He looks back at me with anger in his eyes, or maybe it's just frustration since I'm clearly nothing he wants to deal with. "Sienna, this is your responsibility. I'm tired of fighting you on this. You will do this. You will marry Lucius Angeloni. That's it."

I look up at him as he yanks me by the arm down this hallway. "I'm not fighting you. I just don't need to be treated like some kind of animal. You never had to kidnap me. None of this should have happened."

As we walk, I look at guests as they pass us and wish just one of them would do something to put an end to this madness. Don't any of them wonder why I'm being dragged down this hallway?

Obviously not. Between the drinking and the food and the women barely clothed in tiny bikinis serving all these people, they probably can't even be bothered to notice me.

I look for Alaric, desperate to see his face or Gideon's face. Anyone from the Rule family, but they're nowhere to be found.

Matteo stops in front of a large wooden door at the end of the hallway and turns around to face me, glaring an expression of hatred down at me. "You will go in here, and you will do what you need to. Remember your responsibility is to your family. You abandoned us, and now it's time to right that wrong. Our father died thinking that you had disappointed your family. You can change that now."

I open my mouth to snap that my father died merely disappointed his goddamned hitman hadn't killed me like he ordered, but before I can say another word, Matteo opens the door and shoves me into the room, slamming it shut behind me. I look around and see a bedroom that's decorated nearly entirely in gold. It's completely gaudy. I can't imagine what kind of person would want to sleep in a room like this.

Then again, I know whose room this is. My intended husband's. Lucius Angeloni.

I look around for him, but he doesn't seem to be here. In fact, I seem to be alone. I take a step toward the balcony door.

And then another. And then, I feel a hand touch my shoulder. Oh, God. I spin around and see Lucius standing there staring at me.

He looks so old compared to me right now.

And the first thing that comes into my mind is this man knew my father and now I'm supposed to marry him. To hear my brother talk, he's interested in me. Why? It can't just be because I'm young. There are dozens of young women at this party tonight. Every one of them is beautiful. He could have any one of them.

I've noticed a fair number them eyeing him up like he's a prize. Any one of those women would happily marry him.

So why me?

I know the answer. It has to do with our families joining and power and Matteo taking over where my father left off in his life when he died. I thought I escaped all of that when I got away from here two years ago.

I stare at Lucius and wonder if this is the moment when I'm going to be expected to sleep with him. Terror races through me. I can't sleep with this man. I won't marry this man. Alaric has to find a way to get me out of here.

"Hello, Sienna. Welcome to my bedroom."

I wait for him to reach out and touch me or do anything, but he simply stands there staring at me. Dressed in his black tux, he looks very formal, almost as if this is some kind of costume he wears for occasions like this. I'm not his first wife — I'm not even his first fiancée — so I wonder if this is all choreographed.

I haven't forgotten this is the same man who saw me tied to that chair at the villa and did nothing to help me. He can dress up like a distinguished gentleman with an impressive pedigree all he wants. He's nothing more than a vicious thug, just like my brother.

Lucius stalks around the dimly lit room, never taking his eyes off me. He studies me like I'm some kind of prized possession he's examining now that he's bought me, like another of his Etruscan vases he intends to put in some beautifully lit alcove to show off to all his guests.

If only that were my fate.

"Perhaps we should get to know one another better," he says with a dangerous smile. "Tell me something about you, Sienna Rossetti."

I look into his dark eyes and say the first thing that comes to my head. "I was supposed to graduate the other day. Four years at college for that one day and I didn't get to have that because my brother kidnapped me."

Lucius looks down and then shakes his head, almost as if he feels bad for what happened to me. But he's smiling, a clear sign he doesn't care that the biggest day of my life passed without me getting to enjoy a moment of it.

"That's unfortunate."

That's it. Nothing more. He doesn't ask me what I went to school for or if I did well or anything else. Simply that's unfortunate.

"I knew your father years ago. We were the best of friends when we were around your age."

My skin feels like it's crawling at his mention of being my age and being friends with my father. This is disgusting and wrong. I can't imagine how my brother thinks this is okay for me, but I force a smile because I know I must.

"That's nice," I say quietly in a voice I hope doesn't betray how much he disgusts me right now.

"I remember you around the house when I was younger. I'm glad my father had a friend like you," I say, all lies but needing to keep the conversation going so we don't move to what's about to happen next.

But none of my words mean anything. I just feel like if I stop talking, he's going to want to take this to the bed, and that's the last thing I want to do tonight.

"Your family, the Rossetti family, has a long tradition of being honorable. You should be proud of that, Sienna," Lucius says as he walks over toward the balcony.

I can't help but laugh at the idea that anything about my family is even close to being honorable. Was it honorable for my father to order a hit on me? Was it honorable for my brother to kidnap me and keep me tied to a chair for days? Is it honorable that he's sold me off to this man like a thing that can be handed over to anyone as long as they offer enough money?

In a moment of daring, I reply, "I have nothing really to say about the Rossetti family. I've never felt like one of them, and I don't think they ever felt I was one of them either."

A look of surprise comes over his face. "Even your father? I know he loved you dearly."

Laughter explodes out of me, partly because I'm nervous and partly out of disgust at the thought that my father ever truly cared about me. "Oh yeah, he cared enough to send one of his men to kill me. My father was a son of a bitch, just like my brother."

Lucius's eyes get wide for a moment, but then he shakes his head as if anything I've just said isn't the absolute truth. "That wasn't your father, Sienna. Your father would never put a hit out on you. He would never put a hit out on anyone in his family. Salvatore Rossetti had his many flaws, but he was loyal to his family, if no one else. That wasn't your father. That was your brother."

My entire body begins to shake as I take a step back, forgetting how tight my dress is and how little I can move in it as his claim sinks in. My brother ordered the hit on me? Not my father?

"No, my father did that. The hitman was my father's man," I mutter as all of this rambles around in my head.

Lucius hums and shakes his head again. "Matteo

did that. Your father died not knowing his own son had put a hit out on his only daughter."

My breath catches in my chest at what Lucius is saying. Is he telling the truth? Is this for real? Suddenly, I feel like I'm unsure about so much. I never doubted that my father would have put a hit out on me. I don't know why. He had no reason to hate me that much, but when his man said that to me in that tiny little field before I knelt down with my face in the grass waiting to be shot in the head on my own father's orders, never did I doubt for a second that he had sent him there to kill me.

But now, standing here in this room after hearing Lucius tell me it wasn't my father but my brother who wanted me dead, a feeling of sadness washes over me. I have never mourned my father's death because I never felt he deserved it. Now, for the first time, emotion bubbles up inside me.

My father didn't want me dead.

Lucius steps toward me and brushes his hand along my forearm. "I've got guests to attend to. Take a few minutes. I'm sure finding out the truth about who wanted to kill you that day is jarring. Compose yourself and come out when you're ready but don't take long. My woman is someone who needs to entertain people, and as the lady of this household from tonight on, you will be expected to ensure that my guests are always happy."

I stare up at him in confusion. I've just heard that the person I believed had wanted me dead and put a hit out on me didn't do it, and in fact, it was my brother who sent that man to kill me, and all Lucius Angeloni can talk about is how I'm supposed to cater to his guests and make sure that their wine glasses are filled and they have enough food in their stomachs?

I don't care about any of that. I don't care about him or this wedding he and my brother are so eager to have happen.

When I don't respond, he turns away, walking out the bedroom door and leaving me alone. I can't stay here. I need to get out of this place. I need to get away from him and my family.

Frantic to find a way to escape, I run to the balcony doors and throw them open. The warm night air rushes over me, and as much as I want to believe I'm this close to freedom, I'm still alone. I don't see Alaric. I don't see Gideon. I don't see anyone who can help me.

I look out off the side of the balcony, hoping to see a friendly face somewhere nearby but there's no one. "Alaric," I call out. "Are you there? Are you anywhere nearby?"

The sounds of people enjoying themselves at the party coming from the other side of the house are my only reply. In the distance, the sound of a boat's horn blares into the night. But no Alaric.

Hopelessness fills me, mixing with the sadness I feel about what I just found out about my father. I can't find a way out of this. I burst into tears, covering my face with my hands. I'm going to be trapped in a marriage with this man who's twice my age.

How am I ever going to do this? The man I love has disappeared, and I'm going to marry Lucius Angeloni. God help me.

I walk back into the room hoping to find any way to escape that fate. There is none. I must accept it. Drying my eyes, I walk over to stand in front of a mirror on the far wall. Jesus, I look like a nightmare in this silver dress. I look like a sad hooker.

And then behind me, I see something move. I spin around and there coming through the door I see Alaric.

I run to him, my ankles threatening to roll in these four-inch heels, thrilled to see him there. Wrapping my arms around his shoulders, I hold him close to me as I shake in fear that at any moment Lucius will find me standing here with him.

I inhale a deep breath, filling my nose with the smell of his skin. It's musky and sexy and manly, and it makes me smile as my eyes stay closed and he holds me to him.

"Alaric, did you find a way to get me out of here? He's going to come back at any moment. He's talking about me entertaining his guests and being the woman of the house in here, in this bedroom, which looks like some kind of bizarre old man's sex cave. Oh, God. I can't stay here. Did you find a way for us to get out?"

Alaric gently pushes me away from him and nods. "I've got an idea. We're not the only ones who are looking to make sure that Lucius Angeloni doesn't get what he wants tonight."

I shake my head in confusion. "I don't understand what you mean. We're not the only ones. Are you talking about your cousin Gideon?"

Alaric smiles. "No, there's someone else here tonight who has plans for Lucius. His name is Alexei Wolfe."

Quickly, I try to remember if I've ever heard that name before. Alexei Wolfe. No, it doesn't ring any bells.

"Who is he? Is he going to help us?" I ask, searching Alaric's eyes for any solace from the utter panic that's settled into every inch of me.

The man I love takes my hands in his and brings them up to his lips to kiss my knuckles. "He's like me," he explains.

I stare up into his beautiful dark eyes, still confused. "Like you? Do you mean he's like a Rule? He's one of your family?"

Alaric shakes his head again. "No, he's a hitman like me."

I stare at him, unsure what he's talking about. "A hitman? Is there some kind of union or something you guys all belong to? Are you guys having a meeting here or is this some kind of fraternity you all joined?"

That makes Alaric laugh out loud, and his smile lights up his face. "Not exactly. Our paths cross every so often. Alexei has been in the business a long time, much longer than me. He and his wife live here in

Italy, and his daughter was the most recent woman in Lucius Angeloni's life."

The way he says that makes me concerned that whoever this woman was, she did not fare well in this room and in this house. "Is she dead?" I ask holding back tears. "Did he kill her?"

Sadness fills Alaric's eyes. "She escaped after he beat her almost to within an inch of her life. Now her father has come back to exact his revenge."

"So this hitman is here now to kill Lucius tonight?"

Alaric nods. "Yes, so all we need to do is stay out of his way. Someone else can do this job, and I can get you away safe."

As much as Alaric makes this sound like it's going to be easy, it's not. My brother's going to force me back home if Lucius is dead. "Alaric, there's no way Matteo will simply be okay with me going back to my life. If he doesn't marry me off to Lucius tonight, he'll find someone else. Trust me."

Alaric wraps his strong arms around me and pulls me to him. "Not if I have anything to say about it. You don't belong here. You belong with me."

My cheek rests against his chest, and I hear his heartbeat as I think about all that's happened tonight. Quietly, I tell him what I now know. "Matteo was the one that sent that man to kill me. It wasn't my father. It was my own brother. Lucius just told me that."

I can't believe my own brother wanted me dead.

Alaric holds me gently in his arms and whispers,

"He'll pay for that. I promise Sienna. He'll pay for that."

Payback and revenge are for another time. Tonight, I just want to escape this terrible place with Alaric and return to my life.

CHAPTER FIFTEEN

ienna

I SLOWLY WALK DOWN THE HALLWAY BACK TO THE party, dreading the performance I have to give in a few seconds. I don't want to pretend to be the woman of this house. I don't want to pretend that I care about Lucius Angeloni.

All I want is to be as far away from here as possible with Alaric.

People mill about the room talking and laughing. They have no idea what's going on. They have no idea that tonight I'm going to be sold to the highest bidder because my brother feels nothing for me other than what I'm worth to him.

I take my position next to Lucius, and he glances over at me as if to say I'm doing well and I'm behaving as he expects me to. I force a smile that will remain plastered on my face until I can leave this villa. I don't have any other choice.

Slyly, I scan the room for any sign of Alaric, unsure where he's disappeared to but hoping that at any moment he will do something to get me out of here.

Lucius softly slides his hand around my waist in a sign of pure ownership for the men standing around him. As they talk, I notice this slight movement and acknowledge it with an appreciative gaze up him. At least that's what I hope it looks like and not a death stare from a woman who can't wait to be away from him.

He returns my gaze with one of his own that tells me he feels like some conquering hero claiming his prize. I am no one's prize here. I will not be bought and paid for between men who aren't much better than troglodytes.

I see Gideon over near the doorway to the terrace talking to a dark-haired man around his height. Dressed in a tux like every other man here, he cuts a dashing figure with his chiseled face and sharp gaze. Is that the hitman Alaric was talking about, the one whose daughter Lucius nearly killed? Is he waiting for his chance? I wish he wouldn't wait any longer get rid of this vicious creature who insists on touching me and keeping me pinned to his side.

I want to be free.

The room looks different now that I've spent a few

moments of time alone with Lucius in his bedroom. His home is full of all the trappings of wealth, but it feels like something more is on display here. It isn't just that he has money. It's that he has power.

And he wears his power so everyone knows it.

I can't help but compare him to my father, who never looked like he had as much power as he did. He always looked like that dutiful civil servant, which is I how I imagine people assumed that he was never into all the horrible things he was actually doing.

Out of the corner of my eye, I see my brother beaming a smile. I'm sure he's happy. The transaction is complete. As far as he's concerned, he probably thinks Lucius and I have already had sex.

So now it's just a matter of getting his payment. Fuck him. Before I leave Italy for the last time, I will make sure that my brother understands he made a mistake when he took me from my happy life.

"Lucius, when is the big day?" a man asks, and my attention is immediately focused on him.

I snap my head to look at the man and see he reminds me of my father, a little older than Lucius by a few years, if his gray hair and the wrinkles around his eyes are any indication. The guest eagerly waits for the answer to when our wedding will take place, and unlike most bridegrooms, Lucius never looks over at me as if to say, "When is the big day, sweetheart?"

Why should he, though? That's not what this is about, and everyone in this room knows it. So nobody waits for me to answer. Their attention is entirely focused on him, which is exactly as he wants it to be.

He doesn't seem to be very interested in actually naming a date, so he sidesteps the question, waving his hand with a flourish in the air and giving me a moment's peace and reprieve from his touching me. "Soon enough. Soon enough, the Angeloni and Rossetti families will be joined."

The man nods his head solemnly, as if those words are incredibly meaningful to him. "Sienna's father would have loved to have seen this finally taking place, God rest his soul."

Another man with big eyes full of curiosity asks, "Are you looking to have children this time?"

Oh, God. Who asks that kind of thing at a party? I guess this man views me like everyone else here — merely as an attractive receptacle for Lucius Angeloni's sperm.

"Lucius, it's never too late," he says with a chuckle, as if reproducing is an amusing thing for this person.

My intended husband thinks the question is funny too because he throws his head back and laughs. It explodes out of his throat like it's the most amusing thing he's ever heard in his life.

"Children," he says in a low voice tinged with a hint of disgust. "I don't know about that. The little woman here certainly looks like she can bear children, but perhaps we'll wait a little while."

God, this man is vile. The little woman looks like

she can bear children? Why is that? Do I have hips that indicate I'm fertile? What a pig he is.

My stomach turns at the thought of giving this man a child. He's twice my age to start with. We aren't in love, and I'm being held against my will. Why the hell would I be interested in giving him anything as precious as a child?

As Lucius and his guests coarsely talk about my future and potential reproductive abilities as if I'm not here, suddenly I sense the air around us begin to crackle with excitement. I can't put my finger on why, but it's almost as if everyone is making plans at this moment.

Lucius is talking about our future and children as if I have no say in it. I'm waiting for Alaric to show up. I know that other hitman is somewhere nearby. I see my brother practically salivating at the thought that all his dreams are going to come true tonight. It's like anticipation hangs thick in the air with everyone just waiting for something to happen.

I'm not sure what's about to happen, but all I know is I've never felt so on edge in my life.

Alaric's nowhere to be found, and I watch Gideon for any sign he's nearby, but I see nothing. He continues to speak to that man who I've now decided can't be the hitman. Or maybe he is. I know nothing about being a hitman. Maybe it's customary for them to walk around casually and act like an everyday, average person and then suddenly pull out a gun.

God, I hope somebody gives me fair warning

because I'm standing right next to the man. Someone trained to kill wants to take out Lucius, and all I can think about is how to save myself if all hell breaks loose. Then again, if he or my brother wanted undying loyalty, they should have thought twice about kidnapping me and forcing me to accept a marriage I never wanted.

Out of the corner of my eye, I see someone move through the door to the room. I look over and there is Alaric. In his tux, he looks like he fits in here with all these people. I know better, though. He's nothing like these people surrounding me.

His gaze drifts over me, and I feel my eyes widen as he begins to walk toward where I stand next to Lucius. Frantic at what he plans to do, my heart races. It feels like it's slamming into my rib cage and threatening to explode out of my chest with every step he takes. Why is he coming over here? Is he planning to do something right now?

This can't be his plan. Oh, God! There are security guards everywhere, and my brother and his guards are nearby.

Please, God. Don't let this be Alaric's plan or the two of us might end up dead.

CHAPTER SIXTEEN

laric

SIENNA'S TERRIFIED EXPRESSION FILLS MY EYES AS I stroll past Lucius Angeloni on my way toward the bar. I'm waiting for the exact moment a distraction comes along to set my plan in motion. I know Alexei will create some problem that will work to my advantage. It's just a matter of time.

But for now I'm forced to stand and listen to this son of a bitch talk about how he intends on possibly having children with the woman I love. And how she makes the perfect hostess for his villa. As if Sienna is nothing more than window dressing. The woman has a four-year degree from an Ivy League school, for fuck's sake.

Even I can appreciate that, yet this fuck stands

there talking to his friends as if she doesn't exist at his side except when he wants to make it clear to all of them that this is his new conquest.

Too bad I don't get to kill this one tonight, but he's Alexei's, not mine. My fellow hitman has far more reason to be justified in this kill.

I glance over in Gideon's direction and see him talking to a man and woman who appear to be a couple. She's gorgeous with a great body, long dark hair, and an exotic feel about her. He resembles every other man here dressed in a black tux. He's nothing special, but he does look like he has money.

The woman stands out in comparison. This is the first I've seen her at this party tonight, but she doesn't look like most of the other women here. She isn't dripping with jewels, and I get the sense she isn't as interested in the man next to her as he is in her.

The same can't be said for most of the couples here.

I'm on red alert watching for the moment I can spring into action, and a few minutes later that moment finally comes, strangely enough, not from Alexei but because of Gideon. What appeared to be a polite conversation among him, the man, and the woman erupts suddenly.

"Who the fuck do you think you are? Don't talk to me like that," the man snaps at the woman with him, threatening her.

Every head turns in their direction to see what's

going on, and I can see by the look on my cousin's face that he's instantly uncomfortable. The woman pushes her hands against the man's chest, and a second later, he slaps her hard across the face, sending her tumbling to the ground. I watched stunned as no one does anything, except for Gideon. He steps in between them in an attempt to try to calm things down, but it's no use.

Whatever happened between the three of them, the man is on fire, and he's pissed.

"Who the fuck do you think you are helping her? You don't help her. She's mine. My woman. My property. Mine. If I want to fucking slap her and throw her to the ground, if I want to grind her under my fucking heel, I will," he screams before he shoves Gideon, who nearly falls back into the woman as she struggles to get back on her feet.

But he doesn't want this fight. It's not his style. Putting his hands up in front of him, he calmly says, "There's no fight here. No fight at all. I'm sorry if I offended."

As he crouches down to help the woman up, I look around and see everyone watching this scene, even all the bodyguards and security here tonight. When she finally stands back up on her feet, her boyfriend proceeds to slap her again.

And that's what all hell breaks loose.

Although it's not in my cousin's nature, he launches at the man, taking him to the ground. The woman screams. Punches are thrown. And suddenly everyone at the party is focused solely on them, including Lucius and Sienna.

Now is my chance.

I watch as Gideon and the man get up to their feet and their fight spills out into the garden outside. Lucius, Matteo, and all the other guests, including all the security guards, rush out to see the fight, leaving Sienna alone.

Her eyes are wide and filled with fear when she looks at me. She knows this is our opportunity. I grab her and start running in the opposite direction down a hallway I checked out earlier when I was looking for ways to escape.

From outside in the garden someone yells, "Security! Get out here right now!" That's the gift that I've been waiting for with this distraction. We can simply walk out of this villa scot-free.

Sienna clutches my hand tightly as we rush toward the door on the other end of the home. "Oh my God, Alaric! Did Gideon plan that? Did he do that on purpose? Is that what the plan was?" she asks breathlessly.

As we hurry down the dark hallway toward a door that leads to the other side of the estate, I shake my head. "No, he had no part in this. This isn't Gideon style. He's definitely not someone who starts a fight at a party. Gideon plays it cool. He doesn't brawl like that. I have no idea why he attacked that guy over what happened."

Maybe he was feeling chivalrous? I have no idea.

All I know is I'm thankful for the distraction.

"Well, thank God he did it for whatever reason." Sienna laughs as the side of that terrible silver dress of hers tears all the way up to just underneath her arm. "Oh my god! I just ripped this hideous dress. Everyone's going to see everything now!"

I laugh, looking over at her as she flashes nearly her entire body at me. "Not if I have anything to say about it. Now let's go."

A man appears from through the door where we need to go. For a moment, my heart skips a beat. Is this one person going to be the reason we can't escape? Over my dead body. It's between us and him.

I pull my gun from inside my tux jacket and aim at his chest before he can say a word. The shot takes him out instantly, and he drops like dead weight to the floor ahead of us.

Sienna screams, but I quickly cover her mouth to silence her cries. "Shhh. It was him or us, baby."

She nods as tears fill her eyes. "I know. I just wasn't ready to see you kill him."

Pressing a kiss to her trembling lips, I whisper, "Trust me. I wouldn't do it if I didn't have to."

Sienna looks up at me and tries to smile, but it never actually makes it to the corners of her mouth. "I know. I trust you, Alaric. I trust you with my life."

I scan the area to see if anyone else might get in our way but see no one. With that one obstacle gone, she and I look at each other and know we're free.

I throw the door open and yank her outside with

me into the darkness as the night swallows us up. I've cased out this entire estate. I know exactly how to get away from here now that we're out of the villa.

"Alaric, where are we? Which way do we go?" she asks, her hand tightly squeezing mine.

"I got you. Just follow me."

As we start out across the grounds of Lucius's villa, she sobs, "I can barely run in these shoes. My god, four-inch heels. I can barely move."

I look down on her feet as we're running. "Take them off. Kick them away. You don't need them. I'll buy you new shoes. We'll get lots of new shoes. You can have whatever you want."

She smiles and stops for a moment to kick her left shoe and then her right shoe into the grass. "I never liked those goddamned things. Can you believe my brother thought I should be wearing those shoes? And this dreadful dress? I'd take the dress off too if I could, except then I'd be buck naked."

I quickly take my jacket off and slip it over her shoulders. "Put this on. Nobody needs to see you racing through the streets half naked."

She slides her arms into the sleeves that hang low off her hands. With a smile, she says, "I didn't realize you were so modest, Alaric. What do you care if people see a little skin?"

I look over at her and shake my head as we run moving toward the edge of the Angeloni estate and freedom just steps away. "I care because your mine. I don't need other men seeing you like that. When we get back to the hotel, I'll get you something else to wear."

Barely catching her breath, she says, "I sort of like this whole look I have going on with your tux jacket, to be honest. It's comfortable. A little big. I'm sort of swimming in it, but I think it looks good on me. Don't you think?"

I look forward toward the last few yards before we will leave this villa and the Angeloni estate forever and not at her. "You always look good, Sienna. Always."

The moment we step off Lucius Angeloni's property, I hear Sienna let out a heavy sigh. She knows she's free and she's safe in the darkness. I turn to her, and she throws her arms around me.

"Thank you, Alaric! I wasn't sure how we were going to ever escape from there. Thank you. I can never repay you for this. I owe you my life."

Pulling her to me, the scent of her vanilla shampoo wafts up to my nose as she rests her head on my shoulder. She smells sweet and warm and fresh, just like she always has.

"You owe me nothing. This is what you do when the woman you love needs you."

She lets out another heavy sigh against my chest. "I love you. You saved me when I didn't think we had a chance."

In the distance, someone lets out a blood curdling scream, It's a woman, and she's joined by others a second later before people begin to cry out the words

I've longed to hear from the moment I found out what Matteo planned to do to Sienna.

"Lucius is dead! Someone's killed Lucius!" a chorus of people scream in horror.

While they mourn the loss of the man, I silently rejoice that Alexei was able to avenge his daughter. In our business, it's very rare when you're justified in killing someone. This was more than a job for Alexei, and I'm glad that he got to give Lucius Angeloni what he deserved.

Sienna looks up at me, her eyes wide in fear. "Alaric, that man, that hit man killed Lucius." She sounds so innocent, as if she didn't believe that Alexei would actually do his job.

Cradling her face, I let out a sigh like I've been holding my breath for days. "You're free now. You're free, and your brother is the only one who stands in our way, but that won't be forever. I'll make sure of that."

I see a darkness cross her expression when I say those words, but with a kiss, she's the woman I fell in love with not far from here two years ago. As we hurry off toward Gideon's hotel, I silently pledge that whatever that dark look meant won't get in our way of being happy.

We've been through too much already to not deserve bliss.

CHAPTER SEVENTEEN

laric

HER EYES CLOSED, SIENNA LIES IN THE MIDDLE OF the king size bed in the suite Gideon gave me. From the moment she walked through the door, it's been our room.

Our sanctuary. The one place I know she's safer than anywhere else in the world on this night.

I slip out of my dress shirt and toss it onto the chair in the corner of the room. "You aren't falling asleep on me, are you?"

She smiles and opens her eyes as she shakes her head. "I would have thought after all that happened that I'd be exhausted, but I'm wide awake. I was just reveling in how incredible this bed feels."

Still dressed in that ugly silver dress, although now

it resembles silver tatters more than anything else, she looks more beautiful than every other woman in the world right now. In those moments when I thought I lost her, I silently promised if I had another chance to show Sienna how I feel, I'd make sure I erased those two years without me so she'll never doubt I'm a man crazy in love with her.

"Gideon has a nice place here," I say with a chuckle as I make my way over to the bed as she sighs.

"Nice isn't the word for it," Sienna says with a sexy smile as she rolls back and forth on the mattress from one side to the other. "I don't think I've ever felt such a comfortable bed in my life. It's like I'm lying on a cloud. Your cousin has excellent taste in mattresses."

I stop in front of her and nudge her legs open with my knee. "I'll be sure to tell him. Of all the compliments he's received in his life, I bet this will be the first for his choice of beds."

"Have you slept in this bed yet? Seriously, you need to lie down and tell me this isn't the most comfortable thing you've ever felt in your life."

I let my gaze drift up and down her body and smile. "I'd rather be on top of something else, to be honest."

That gets me an odd look, and a second later, Sienna slides off the bed to stand in front of me. "I need to get out of this asinine dress," she says, looking down her body at the strips of silver fabric hanging from just under her ribs. "I guess it's not actually a dress anymore. It's more like a silver version of those things at the car wash."

She lifts her arms and smiles up at me with such innocence that it feels wrong to be thinking of how much I want to be inside her. "Help me get this ugly thing off. It needs to go in the garbage, where it belonged in the first place."

I tug it up over her head in one hard yank and toss it over toward the wastebasket near the desk on the other side of the room. When I turn back to face her, she's standing naked in front of me and looking like some kind of goddess.

"My brother didn't bother to give me underwear or a bra when he insisted I wear that ridiculous get-up," Sienna says with uncharacteristic shyness, avoiding my gaze.

"Don't think about him or that ugly thing he made you wear," I say with a smile as I tilt her chin up so she looks at me.

Her dark eyes look unsure, but I don't know why. Hoping to reassure her that she's safe from now on, I lean down to press a soft kiss against her lips.

"It's okay, Sienna. I won't let him or anyone hurt you ever again. I promise."

She tries to give me a smile, but it never reaches her eyes still full of something that says she's worried. "I know."

"Then what's wrong? I can see it in your eyes. Something's bothering you. What is it? Tell me."

A heavy sigh escapes from her, and her shoulders

sag like she's been carrying the weight of the world for far too long. "I think it's just everything. Being taken from my home right before graduation. Sitting in that room at my brother's for all those hours. Then finally having to go through all of that tonight. I honestly think that's why I was raving about the bed. It's the first time I've felt safe since right after you left my apartment the other day."

Taking her beautiful face in my hands, I cradle it as I try to imagine how traumatizing all of that was for her. I have the ability to compartmentalize — I always have — and that makes dealing with things easier. I see something I need to overcome, so I do whatever I have to in order to make that happen.

But that's because I'm the one in control. When I'm not, life becomes almost impossible to deal with.

Sienna hasn't had any control from the moment that fucker Trent grabbed her and handed her over to her brothers. I can't even imagine how hard it's been for her.

That's all over now, though. She's with me, and I won't let anything happen to her ever again.

"I'm sorry I wasn't there so none of this happened. From now on, if someone wants to get to you, they'll have to get through me first. You know that, right?"

"I do. I guess it's everything happening that's got me a little frazzled and getting rid of that dress I hated from the moment he forced me to put it on just made everything come into focus, Alaric. I don't know what

I would have done if you didn't show up at that party tonight."

With a smile, I press a tiny kiss to her forehead and whisper against her soft skin, "You never have to think that again, Sienna."

She sighs and hangs her head. I wait for her to begin crying, but she doesn't. Instead, she takes a deep breath in and lets it out in a rush, as if she's tired of feeling bad.

"Thank you, but I'm not sure I'll ever forget what my brother did. I know you probably think tonight and all those days I was tied to that chair were what's bothering me, but even worse than that is that he took away something important to me I'll never get the chance to experience."

With tears in her eyes, she looks up at me and blows the air out of her lungs. "I was looking forward to graduation day. I worked so hard to graduate with honors, and he took that away without a single thought."

"I'm sorry. I know that meant the world to you."

Sienna practically collapses onto the bed, sitting on the edge like she can't stand a moment longer. "It did. When I changed schools from Brown to Yale, I wasn't sure I'd be able to do it. Everyone thinks I'm so smart, but that kind of change isn't something that always works out."

As I sit down next to her, I tell her something I've never said to anyone in the two years I didn't see her. "I wish I was there all that time. I never thought you'd have a problem adjusting, but now I'm thinking it wasn't as easy for you as I imagined."

When she turns to look at me, I see how happy my being there would have made her. "I would have liked to have you there with me, Alaric. I missed you."

"You don't have to miss me anymore. I'm right here on this bed that feels like a cloud."

That makes her giggle, and her cheeks turn a sweet shade of pink. "It does, doesn't it?"

"I think we should see if this cloud can handle the two of us together."

Sienna smiles broadly and shakes her head. "I have this image of angels having sex on a cloud."

I snake my arm around her waist and lean back onto the bed, pulling her down on top of me. As she stares into my eyes, I wink at her. "I'm no angel."

Rolling her hips, she presses her bare pussy to my hard cock still covered by my tux pants. "I'm not sure I am either."

My eyes flutter closed as the feel of her body rubbing against mine sends delicious sensations rolling through me. God, I've missed this. I told myself I could live without this—live without her. I rationalized that she deserved to have a chance at the life of her dreams, and I couldn't be part of that.

I wanted her to be happy, but I was lying to myself. I need her in my life.

My hands skim down over her body, sure of their way because I memorized every inch of her that first time we were together. Her sides that are so ticklish that she snickers when my fingertips graze her skin. Her hips that flare out from her waist, womanly and beautiful. Her ass that I love to cup in my hands.

The feel of her petal-soft skin against my palms makes me wish my hands didn't have callouses. She deserves better than the roughness I offer. Still, she doesn't cringe when I touch her, instead urging me on with her gentle sighs and needy moans with every inch I caress.

"Is something wrong?" she whispers, and I open my eyes to see concern written all over her face.

I shake my head and smile. "Nothing except the look on your face. Not exactly what a man hopes to see when he has a naked woman on top of him."

Sienna rolls her eyes. "I look like this because you seemed to be a million miles away there for a minute. Your eyes were closed, and it felt like you touched my ass and something made you stop. What's wrong?"

"Nothing. I was just thinking how much I love your body. I thought I memorized every inch of it the first time we had sex, but tonight feels like you're brand new to me again."

Her eyes grow wide with appreciation. "Really? I like that. It's so romantic."

Tilting my hips up, I push my hard cock against her pussy and grin. "I've got something else you might like."

"So much for romance."

She bites her lip, a clear sign that while she may want romance, she also wants what I'm rubbing against her. Leaning down, she kisses me long and deep and says, "Then again, I'm not sure there's anything more romantic than a man rescuing a damsel in distress like you did for me tonight."

"That's me. Riding in on my white horse to save the day."

Sienna's eyebrows shoot up into her forehead in disbelief as she slides her palms down my chest to unbutton my pants. "White horse? Are you the same man who kidnapped a damsel in distress one time?"

As she reaches under my pants to palm my cock, I smile at her description of me. "Only once. I promised said damsel I'd never do that again."

She tugs my pants down my legs and tosses them onto the floor before climbing back on top of me. This time, her wet pussy rests along my hard shaft, teasing me with what's to come.

Her expression serious, she steadies herself with her palms on my chest and sighs. "I didn't think you'd take that to mean not sleeping with anyone while we weren't together, Alaric. I love that you didn't, though."

I pull her mouth down to mine and kiss her like I wanted to all night at that bastard's house. "Once you have the one you want, it's impossible to look at anything else and think you're willing to take a pale substitute. I only wanted you."

"For such a bad man, you say some wonderful things."

She rolls her hips again, and this time I slide inside

her. It feels like heaven on earth, just as it always does with Sienna. I could stay in this bed with her for the rest of time and never miss a thing in the outside world because I'd have her.

Stuffing my hand in her hair, I pull her body down to mine so her breasts press against my chest. In this position, I have the perfect angle to do what I want.

When the first finger slips into her ass, she makes a noise like she's both surprised and happy. Our bodies begin to move faster so in only a minute she's practically bucking against me and riding my cock for all it's worth.

I take that as the cue that she wants more, so I let a second finger join the first. She's as tight as can be, but if she ever wants to take my cock in her ass, she's going to need to be trained first.

Sienna's head pops up from where she's been kissing my neck with the initial thrust of both fingers inside her, and the look in her eyes tells me her surprise isn't joined exactly by happiness now.

"No…Alaric…it's too much," she says as she shakes her head.

"You sure?"

I leave both fingers inside her, still but filling her completely. Knitting her eyebrows, she answers my question with a frown and says, "Yes. It's too much. I'm sorry."

With that, I slide them out of her ass and roll her over onto her back, my cock staying inside her. "It's okay. I have something that might help that."

Reaching over to the nightstand, I open the drawer and pull out the gift I bought her. She lets out a gasp when I lift it up for her to see.

"Do you routinely carry butt plugs around?" she asks as she stares wide-eyed at the silver and pink jeweled gift I picked up at a store right here on the coast.

I have to stifle a laugh at her question. "No. I thought about the training I told you we'd need to do if you were ever to take me in the ass, so I grabbed this the other day."

Sienna covers her face and laughs. "Oh, my God! You went to that store about a mile down the coast. The adult store my friends and I used to want to go to when we were teenagers. Does that old woman who wears the really red lipstick still work there?"

Nodding as I remember a woman who looked to be about sixty with bright red lipstick at the register, I say, "I'm pretty sure she's the one who sold me this."

"You and the old sex shop woman conspiring to make anal happen with me. Now I can say I've seen everything."

She falls silent for a moment before reaching her hand out. "Well, let me see this thing that's about to know me intimately."

I place it in the center of her palm and watch as she holds it out in front of her, staring at it like it's a bug she isn't sure she wants to let closer to her. "It's okay if you don't want to use it tonight. It's probably bad timing anyway after all you've been through."

When I move to take it from her, she pulls her hand back so I can't. "Let's not be hasty here. I just need a few moments to get acquainted with it. It's sort of cold, but it's getting warmer in my hand."

She's adorable like this. Turning it over in her palm, she examines it and then smiles up at me. "I like the pink jewel thing on the end."

"The choice was pink or purple. I thought you were more of a pink woman."

Suddenly, she frowns and looks away. "I'm sorry. You must think I'm some kind of prude because this is the first time I've ever had one of these in my hand."

I gently turn her face toward me and shake my head. "Not at all. For what it's worth, this is the first one I've ever bought."

"But you've…"

Sienna doesn't finish her sentence, but I know what she meant to say. I've fucked other women in the ass. I don't want her thinking about that, though. That was my past. Whatever I did with those women means nothing to me now that I have the woman I love.

"I'll put it away. We can try it some other time."

With a look of utter resolution, she shakes her head. "No. We'll try it tonight. Just do me a favor, okay?"

"Anything."

As she sets it in my hand, she says in a quiet voice, "Just remember I'm a newbie, okay? No pulling some porn star thing. I'd like to be able to enjoy sex with you in all sorts of ways, but that won't happen if this thing hurts so much that I never want to do it again."

I lean down to kiss her tenderly, utterly charmed by how sweet she can be. Against her lips, I whisper, "I promise. No porn star thing."

That gets me a timid smile. She doesn't have to worry. I would never hurt her. I don't give a damn if she ever wants to have sex this way. All I care about is making her happy.

CHAPTER EIGHTEEN

ienna

UNSURE ABOUT WHAT'S GOING TO HAPPEN NEXT BUT not wanting to shy away from this experience with Alaric, I try not to let my fear get the best of me. I trust him, so whatever happens, I just hope it isn't painful or embarrassing.

"I'm going to roll you onto your stomach."

I look at him, already hating how this has changed the dynamic between us. "You don't have to give me a play-by-play, Alaric. You've never warned me ahead of time when we changed sexual positions before."

Sheepishly, he admits that I'm right. "True. I just didn't want to scare you."

Desperately needing to lighten the mood, I glance down his body to his erect cock pressed against his lower stomach. I reach out and stroke it, smiling. "I'd be scared if you were trying to put this in my ass. That little silver and pink number should be fine."

Alaric gives me a sexy smile that makes me want him in whatever way he likes. "Got it. Back to the way we always are."

The words are barely out of his mouth before he flips me over onto my stomach and presses his hard cock against my ass. In my ear, he moans low and deep and says, "I've wanted you all night."

The timbre of his voice hints at his desire and need, and my pussy runs wet with anticipation. His hands grasp my hips and pull me up to my knees so I'm in the perfect position for him to fuck me. I arch my back, dying to feel him fill me up.

It only takes one hard thrust and he's inside me completely. Alaric groans as he stays still for a long moment, his cock filling me like we were made for one another.

I'm impatient and push back against him, eager for the moment when he begins fucking me in earnest. All my apprehension about the butt plug disappears as I wait for him to move inside me.

His fingers press hard into the flesh around my hips as he slowly slides out of me, only to thrust forward, filling me to the hilt once more. The feeling takes my breath away it's so good, and I don't have to wait long before he begins to move in a satisfying rhythm that makes my body feel like it's more alive than it's ever been.

Need bites at me, and I push back against him as we work to find a cadence to our fucking. It doesn't take long until my pushes are matching his thrusts and he's touching a part of me that no one else in the world has ever reached.

"Oh...God...just like that..." I moan when he pumps into me faster and faster.

He slides his hand around my neck and squeezes gently, thrilling me even more with his power. In my ear, he groans, "Fuck, you feel perfect, like always, baby."

I don't know if it's the way he says those words or the words themselves, but something about them makes me feel like I'm melting. I lower my head to flick my tongue against his thumb near my jaw. His skin is rough and tastes slightly salty, and he moves his hand so his finger presses against my lips. It's an invitation I can't deny, and I suck on it, my tongue worshipping it very much like when I'm on my knees with his cock in my mouth.

Behind me, he makes a guttural sound that goes straight to my pussy, and a moment later, his other hand grabs my hair and tugs my head back hard. It's animalistic and thrills me more than I thought possible after all I've been through.

He pumps his cock into me hard and fast, like he's a man with only one thing on his mind. I understand that, though. All I want at this moment is to come.

As if he can read my mind, Alaric slows his pace until he practically teasing me. I try to push back against him, but he stops me by tightening his hand around my throat.

"Patience. I'm not done with you yet."

I don't know what that means, but I'm desperate to find out, so I try to turn my head to look at him, but he won't allow that either. "Eyes forward," he commands.

Unwilling to fight him on this, even though I want him to fuck me faster, I obey, but not without first telling him what I need. "Please don't tease like this, Alaric."

"Nobody's teasing," he says with what I'm sure is a wicked grin.

He leans down next to my ear and in a low, sexy voice says, "Ready for our new toy?"

His cock still fills my pussy completely, but hearing that, all I want is to see what it will feel like when that silver plug with the pretty pink jewel is inside me. I nod my head to answer his question and feel the bed shift beneath me.

A second later, the smooth tip of the plug presses against my ass and I take a sharp breath into my lungs in surprise. Afraid he'll take that as fear, I say, "I'm ready."

My eyes slowly close as he slowly pushes the entire thing into me inch by inch. At first, it hurts a little, but not as much as his two fingers like before. After a few seconds, the stinging fades away and with the first thrust of his cock deep inside me, a wave of utterly incredible sensations race through my body.

"Oh…God…that feels so damn good…" I say into the pillow as my hands tightly grasp at the sheets.

He moves quicker with every thrust into me, finally giving me what I so desperately crave. His hands squeeze my ass, making the butt plug feel tighter with every pump of his cock. It's almost too much to deal with. My emotions swing from need to desire to momentary fear when I think he's about to take that thing out of my ass and replace it with the monster that hangs between his legs.

I turn to tell him no, but my orgasm tears through me at that very moment, making any thoughts of saying no to him impossible. He could ask me for anything in this world right now, and I'd agree I feel so incredible.

Alaric makes a noise I recognize, and a short time later as my release is winding down, he floods my body with warmth. His cock twitches inside me, pressing against my walls and making it feel like he's growing bigger with every time he comes.

I want to cry out in ecstasy, to tell him how unbelievable that was, but when he presses his fingertip to that pretty pink jewel and puts pressure on the plug, another orgasm rushes through me, taking me by surprise. Finally, my voice returns, and I let out a sob that sounds like it's coming from the depths of my soul.

"Alaric…Jesus, don't stop!"

He tugs on my hair, sending a mixture of pain and pleasure racing across my scalp, and I arch my back, loving the angle that gives his cock. He's still hard inside me, and when I push against him to let him know I'm happy to keep going, he takes the hint and begins pumping into me again.

My body is exhausted, and I'm not sure my arms or legs can hold me up for much longer, but I wouldn't give up this chance to come again for a million dollars. It doesn't take me long to feel that delicious sensation begin to unfurl deep inside me, and when I come for the third time, I'm left without enough strength to hold myself up anymore.

Collapsing onto the bed, I instantly miss him inside me. When I look back behind me, I see him smiling as he strokes his cock.

"I'd do that for you, but I don't think I can lift my arms right now," I say with a giggle.

I watch in rapt attention as he jerks himself off. He's so sensual, happy to pleasure himself while I look on like he's some god of sex thrilled to put on a show.

When he finishes, he lies down next to me and slides his arm around my waist to pull me to him. Our bodies are sweaty and tired, but what's most important isn't the satisfaction we've given one another.

It's that we're together. After all that's happened and all that could have happened tonight, Alaric and I are together again.

I pull his hand up under my chin and revel in the warmth of his skin against mine. "I love how you're always so hot."

He chuckles behind me before softly kissing my shoulder. "Hot as in good looking?"

God, he can be so cute sometimes.

Turning to look at him, I shake my head. "Well, you are good looking, but I'm talking about how warm your skin always is. I noticed it that first time we were together."

"I guess I'm just hot-blooded."

"Well, I love it."

Alaric kisses me softly on the shoulder again and then nuzzles my neck. "I love you, Sienna. Hot or cold, I love you."

I close my eyes and let the happiness I feel wash over me. He loves me. The man who changed my life and who's saved me more than once loves me.

And I love him.

"Can we stay here forever?"

He chuckles, thinking I'm joking. I'm not. I don't want to be in Italy. I just want to be with him right here and never leave so this feeling of utter happiness never goes away.

Rolling over to face him, I kiss his lips and smile. "I'm not entirely serious about staying in this hotel forever. I just don't want to ever stop feeling the way I do right now."

I see a twinkle in his eyes, so I quickly add, "And I'm not talking only about the sex, which was great."

"Are you talking about how you've still got the butt plug in?" he asks, trying very hard to not laugh.

Stunned I didn't remember that, I reach around

and feel the jewel facet between my cheeks. "Oh, my God! I do. Is it going to cause an issue because it's still in there? Alaric, if I have to go to the emergency room here, I'm going to die of embarrassment!"

He kisses me to stop my talking, and I calm down a little. "It's perfectly okay if it stays in. It's supposed to help you get used to feeling something there, so it's fine. No need to go to the ER."

"I want you to know I think you're making fun of me right now," I say, sulking. "I'm sorry I don't know the ins and outs of butt plugs."

Alaric presses his lips together to stop himself from reacting, but it's no use. A laugh explodes out of him. "Do you say things like that intentionally to make me laugh? The ins and outs of butt plugs?"

"Don't make fun of me because I spend more time reading books and less time watching porn. Some people like a woman who hasn't done everything under the sun. It gives the person she's with a chance to introduce her to things."

He pulls me close and places a gentle kiss on my forehead that soothes my hurt feelings. "I'm not making fun of you. I think it's great that I get to do things with you that you've never done with any other man. I'm sorry if you thought I was laughing at you. I swear I wasn't, Sienna."

"Okay."

I curl up against him, pressing my face against his neck and loving how masculine he smells. Like soap and sex all rolled into one Alaric scent.

"We can stay here until you want to leave. Nobody can get to you here. We can get room service, and we can live in this bed for as long as you want," he whispers softly above me.

"What if I want something that isn't on the menu?" I say with a chuckle.

"Then I'll go find it or I'll tell Gideon to get his chef to learn a new recipe."

I lean away to look up at him and the love I see in his expression takes my breath away. "You would, wouldn't you?"

"Of course I would. That's what you do when you love someone."

"Thank you, Alaric."

With a smile, he shakes his head. "No need to thank me."

All of a sudden, I feel so tired, like I can't keep my eyes open anymore. A terrible night followed by a wonderful time with Alaric has led to me feeling utterly exhausted, and all I want to do is fall asleep in his arms.

He seems to sense that because he pulls me close and holds me against him, almost as if to say, "Rest. I'm here, so you never have to worry again."

Alaric Rule, a hitman who kidnapped me, protected me again tonight. I owe him my life. I intend on paying him back the only way I know how.

By loving him for the rest of my life.

CHAPTER NINETEEN

ienna

I OPEN MY EYES AND LOOK UP AT ALARIC TO SEE HIM staring down at me. With a smile, I joke, "I know a lot of people say they'd love someone to watch them sleep, but to be honest, I think it might be a little creepy."

"So much for my being romantic, huh?"

Shrugging, I snuggle up against his side. His skin is so warm, like every inch of him is alive. It's one of the first things I fell in love with about Alaric.

"Why were you watching me?" I ask as I trail my fingertips across his muscular abs.

"No reason," he answers in a quiet voice. "Just woke up and there you were with your head on my chest, so I started watching you sleep."

"I hope I didn't snore. Very unsexy, the snoring thing."

When I look up at him, he shakes his head. "Not that I could tell. For a few minutes, you looked like you were smiling, though. That was pretty cute."

"Uh-oh. We've entered the cute faze of the relationship," I say in a faux worried voice.

But Alaric doesn't seem to get my humor on this and simply stares down in confusion at me. "The cute faze? What's that?"

I don't know if he just doesn't have experience with relationships or he truly has never had one move into the cute faze. He's never told me about anyone before me, so either possibility could be true.

Prepared to take my joke further, I sit up and tug the sheet with me to cover my naked body. He watches me carefully, like he isn't sure what's happening but curious to see what I'll say.

"The cute faze is when everything begins to settle in between two people and things stop being sexy," I explain quite seriously, like I've done actual research on my idea.

He plays along, nodding his head like he's genuinely considering my theory. Knitting his eyebrows, he hums and then says, "Sounds like a demotion to me, so no more cute. I'll have to come up with another way to describe you smiling in your sleep."

With a shrug, I tease, "Well, charming is always nice. I think I'd like to be thought of as charming. I can't say I ever have been that, but I could live with charming."

Alaric leans forward to kiss me sweetly on the lips while his hand tugs at the sheet I'm holding just below my collarbone. "Charming it is then."

His dark eyes gaze into mine when he pulls away from our kiss, and I can't believe how beautiful he is first thing in the morning. I likely look like someone took a hand mixer to my hair, but he's perfect, as always.

"You know, you have to tell me the secret of how you wake up looking pretty much the same as when you went to bed."

Sitting back against the headboard, he runs his hand over the top of his head. "No idea. It's not like I have a lot of hair to do much while I sleep, though, so that's probably it."

Instinctively, I pat my hair against my head, sure it's a disaster. "As opposed to me, who has this mess."

He reaches out to gently touch the ends of my hair hanging down over my breasts and smiles. "I think your hair looks like this more because of the sex we had last night than from sleeping, Sienna. You barely move all night once you close your eyes."

"How would you know since you were asleep?" I ask with a chuckle.

"I sleep very lightly. I wake up a bunch of times during the night, so I see you sleeping. Trust me. You sleep like a rock."

"You must be exhausted all the time then. I know I would be if I woke up during the night."

"Not usually," he says, shaking his head. "I'm used to it. I think I've always been that way. Some people barely fall asleep, while others sleep like the dead."

His smile lights up his face as he says that, and I know he's teasing me. "Like the dead? Well, I guess you'd be the one to know about that."

As soon as the words leave my mouth, I regret them. Never before have I ever said anything against what Alaric does for a living. I know what he is, and I accept that.

At least I thought I did.

He doesn't react immediately to my offhand comment, but slowly I see a look of understanding fill his eyes. I want to apologize, to say I didn't mean anything by that and I have no idea why those words even entered my head.

But I don't get the chance to before he silently slips out of bed, leaving me sitting alone and missing him.

He disappears into the bathroom while I beat myself up over being so insensitive. Alaric is a killer. He's never pretended to be anything but what he is. The idea that I should be making value judgments about what he does after he rescued me from my brother and Lucius Angeloni is offensive, to say the least.

I owe Alaric my life more than once. I have no right to judge him.

When he returns to the hotel room, he's still naked, so I lift the sheet up to welcome him back to bed. He shakes his head, though, and grabs his pants off the chair near the balcony doors.

"We need to make some decisions today, Sienna. We need to get some breakfast and then deal with the problems at hand."

Unsure what he means, I stare across the room at him as I wait for him to explain. When he doesn't, as he slips his shoes on, I ask, "What do you mean? What problems?"

Seated on the dark blue chair that matches the navy-blue curtains keeping the sun out, he lifts his head and answers, "The problem of your brother. That has to be handled. In fact, I'd say they all need to be dealt with. Nip any issues in the bud before they get to be something."

My brother? I have no love for Matteo, or any of my other brothers for that matter, but is he talking about what I think he is?

"What are you saying?" I ask as my hands begin to tremble.

Alaric stands up and walks over toward the closet. Grabbing a white dress shirt, he slides into it, leaving it hanging open as he moves across the room toward me again. "I'm saying you'll never be safe as long as your brother's alive."

Guilt over my father's death courses through me, making what Alaric's saying difficult to hear. I know why he did it, but now that I've found out the truth about who ordered the hit on me that day, I can't help but wonder if I should have found some way to keep Alaric from doing his job when it came to my father.

I know it's silly to think that since I didn't know then and neither did Alaric, but I can't help but feel I'm to blame for my father's untimely death. I shouldn't give a damn what happens to Matteo or any of my brothers. It was him who sent that man to kill me, that son of a bitch. And then he compounded his crimes against me by kidnapping me from my home and dragging me back here to marry that fuck Lucius.

Still, the idea of simply killing the rest of my family feels wrong.

When I don't say anything, Alaric walks over to me and stands next to the bed, staring down into my eyes like he doesn't understand my silence or lack of enthusiasm for what he's implying. "What's wrong?"

I reach out to wrap my fingers around his pinky and force a smile as I shake my head. "Nothing. Nothing's wrong. I'm still a little sleepy, I guess."

"Okay. Then let's get going and handle what we have to do before we set off for home."

As much as I love the idea of leaving Italy, I'm reluctant to move. Alaric waits for me to respond, and when I don't, he backs away from me.

"Sienna, what's going on here?"

Suddenly, I feel defensive. Clutching the sheet under my chin, I look away, unable to face him. "Nothing. Nothing's going on."

"Then why do I get the sense that you think I'm wrong for saying your family needs to be taken care of? First there was that little crack about me being the one to know all about the dead, and now you seem to be acting like the thought of me doing what I need to with your brothers upsets you. What's going on?"

God, the way he's talking about killing people not fifteen minutes after waking up feels so wrong!

"Nothing's going on! Why do you keep asking that?" I cry, far louder and more emotional than I would have liked at this moment.

His eyes stare down at me coldly. "Because I'm getting the feeling you don't understand what needs to happen here."

"I understand fine, thank you," I answer, turning my head so I don't have to see his emotionless stare aimed at me.

"Then you're unhappy about it. Or maybe you don't want to accept that this is how things have to go."

Every word out of his mouth sounds so clinical now that I want to scream. Killing someone's entire family should require some emotion, shouldn't it?

"Sienna, he's going to try to do it again, and next time, he may actually get you married off to some guy. I won't let that happen. You're mine, so you won't be marrying some asshole of your brother's choosing."

I snap my head back to face him. "I'm yours? So I'm the reason all these people have to die? I can't live with that, Alaric."

"You're not the reason. Matteo is the reason Matteo is going to die. I don't understand you. He kidnapped you, sold you to the highest bidder, and now you feel some kind of familial ties that make you feel bad he has to pay?"

"I know what he did!" I say as I jump up from the bed to storm away to the bathroom. "I don't need to be reminded of it. Trust me. I sat there in that room tied up for days. I'll never forget that."

For the second time this morning, I instantly regret the words coming out of my mouth. This time I stop and immediately apologize, though.

"That's not what I'm referring to, in case you think I am."

Alaric's gaze is nothing short of icy as he practically glares at me. "I wasn't thinking it was, but clearly you were in some way."

"This isn't about what happened with us. Don't make it about that. This is about my brother."

"And how you don't want to accept the reality that he needs to be dealt with," Alaric says flatly.

"Tell me. Do you plan on killing my entire family? Is that how it is?"

He simply shakes his head, as if he cannot fathom what my problem is. "Sienna, your brothers will hunt you down, and next time, I might not be able to save you in time. Why do you feel anything for them? They kidnapped you. Sold you to a man whose penchant for hurting women is legendary up and down this coast.

What more do they have to do for you to understand they won't stop until they get what they want?"

Tears well in my eyes, but I steel myself from crying. I will not become an emotional mess about this. I know Alaric's right about my family. I know it, but the way he so blithely talks about having to get rid of them like they aren't human beings isn't something I can understand.

"I don't feel anything for them. Or maybe I do because I'm a stupid woman who gets emotional over stupid things. They're all I have, though. Without them, I have no family at all."

That makes his expression soften, and he walks over to me to cradle my face in his strong hands. "You have me. You have the Rules. You're never alone. I promise that."

As much as his words should make me happy, they only create more questions in my mind. What does he mean I have him? Are we together like a normal couple now, or does he plan on depositing me back at my apartment and visiting me every couple years?

I cover his hands with mine and stare up into his eyes to find the answer, but I can't see anything in them, so I'm forced to ask. "What do you mean I have you? What does that mean, Alaric? You left me alone for two years. You say I'm never alone, but when I was waiting all that time for you, I can tell you I was definitely alone."

Now he seems to have nothing to say, which I

guess is my answer. Backing away from him, I shake my head. "So I'm never alone, but I really am because this little time together is just a vacation from you staying away from me until you decide it's time to pop in and say hi."

That's not fair, and I know it. Alaric hasn't said we're going to return to life as it was for the past two years, but if he's not going to tell me what he wants us to be, I have no choice but to come to the conclusions his silence offers.

"I stayed away from you because I thought you deserved the chance to have the life you deserved."

"Fine. Then the family you claim I have in the Rules—do you mean the group of people who left me alone for two years?" I snap, angry with myself more than with him right now.

"I mean the family that made sure you went to school, had a safe place to live, and wanted for nothing. That family."

His words make me stop short, and I take a deep breath to calm myself, but it doesn't work. "Wanted for nothing? I was alone! I wanted you, Alaric!"

For a moment, it's like the world stops rotating on its axis after my outburst, but then he pushes past me, mumbling, "You weren't alone, Sienna. Remember Trent, the boyfriend who fucking sold you out to your brother?"

I watch him walk away from me, wanting so much to say something to stop him. I don't, though, and when he slams the door behind him, all I feel is regret.

I knew who Alaric was from the first day I met him. He never promised me anything, yet he's given me more than I ever dreamed of.

Maybe the reality is, though, that people like us don't get happily ever afters.

CHAPTER TWENTY

laric

FULL OF BLINDING RAGE, I STORM DOWN TO THE lobby to find Gideon. Maybe it's not rage. I'm not angry with Sienna. I just don't understand for the life of me why she would have any loyalty to a group of people who have no problem selling her off to the likes of Lucius Angeloni.

It's as if she insists on believing her brothers won't do the same thing again and again if I don't do my fucking job. I'm trying to make sure we can be together, and she's worried about losing people who don't give a damn about her.

As if any of those asshole brothers of hers see her in the same way. My family cares more about her than any of the Rossettis.

By the time I reach the main floor, I'm even angrier than when I walked out of the hotel room. Looking around for someone to get me a goddamned cup of coffee, I see not a single soul in the lobby. Where the hell is everyone who works here?

Throwing open Gideon's office door, I walk in to see him sitting behind his desk like he does every day, but one glance tells me something's different this morning. Is that a black eye he's sporting?

"You look like you went ten rounds with someone who kicked your ass. I didn't realize that guy connected with your face."

Gideon winces and lets out a heavy sigh. "My face. My ribs. My fucking kidneys. I guess the only consolation is I think I fucked him up worse. At least I hope I did. This is why I don't fight. I feel like shit this morning."

I glance at the chair in front of his desk and decide to pace instead to work off some of my anger. "Fuck fighting. Kill or don't, but that bullshit slapping someone around is for the birds."

Gideon doesn't respond to my personal mantra but watches me walk back and forth across his office for a few seconds before saying, "What the hell has got you in such a bad mood today? I would have thought you'd be on Cloud Nine this morning. You got the girl, the bad guy got offed, and you got to spend the night in bed with said girl in one of my best suites. Sounds like you should be floating on air, if you ask me."

Stopping directly in front of him, I snap, "Well, I fucking didn't."

"And you're here in my office for what reason then? Because if I don't get to comment on your perfect life, I don't see what the hell we're doing here, to be honest."

Leave it to Gideon to bring things into focus. I do have a pretty damn good life. I'm crazy in love with a gorgeous and intelligent woman who I think is in love with me, and other than the little issue with her family, life looks to be only getting better now that we're together. I guess I shouldn't be stomping around his five-star hotel like someone pissed in my breakfast.

Finally interested in sitting, I pull out the leather chair in front of his desk and practically collapse into it. "Fine, I have a perfect life. Feel free to comment away."

"You might want to tell your face," Gideon says with a chuckle that makes him wince when his ribs start hurting again.

"Sienna doesn't want me to handle her brothers. We had a fight. I'm not sure what she thinks is going to happen if I let them continue to live. I mean, they already kidnapped her and nearly forced her to marry that Angeloni fuck. What makes her think they won't do it again?"

My cousin shrugs. "The fact that they're her family?"

His answer makes me feel even more deflated than I did a second ago when I admitted that she and I had a fight. "Now you sound like her. Exactly how does anyone look at that bunch of assholes and think they're family after what they did?"

"Alaric, you know how families are. Look at ours, for God's sake. Our fathers haven't spoken in decades, but I'm willing to bet all the money I have in that safe over there on the wall that if my father heard there was someone going after Maddox Rule or your father heard there was someone going after Helix Rule, neither one of them would feel good about it. They might not actively work to stop whatever was going to happen, but they wouldn't rejoice in it either. Sienna's family isn't great, but it's all she has. I'm not surprised she doesn't want to see you get rid of them."

"Jesus, did you and Sienna confer about this whole family issue while I was sleeping last night? She said pretty much the same thing about her brothers. They're not great, but they're all she has. I don't get it. Cut them loose and let me take care of business so we can have a happy life. The other choice means we'll always be looking over our shoulders for the rest of our lives. I'm not prepared to live like that."

Wincing from pain, Gideon gingerly leans back in his chair a few inches and levels his gaze on me. "Are you prepared to live without her then? Because that seems to be the choice in front of you."

The mere thought of life without Sienna makes my chest hurt. "Hell, no, I'm not prepared to do that. I'm thinking what's behind Door C is what needs to happen."

"And what's that?"

"I convince her of the reality of the situation, and she agrees."

That makes him laugh, which is quickly followed by more wincing and a low groan. "I know you like to think you can make things happen by sheer force of will, but this might not be one of those times."

"I've got a forty-five that says otherwise."

Gideon rolls his eyes at the mention of my gun. "Are you planning on using it on Sienna? I think you're going to have to come up with some other solution to this problem."

For a moment, I let my mind drift back to that first time we were together after using my gun on Sienna in a way I'd never used a gun before. As insane as it is, I think that was a simpler time for us. There were no families. Just Sienna and me in that villa. It wasn't exactly perfect, but it had its charm.

"I think you're too logical," I say with a laugh.

He shakes his head like I'm making no sense. "I'm a businessman. Logic is an important part of my day-to-day life. You want the flipside of me? Go find my brother."

I don't need to give that offer much thought. "No, thank you. Alex is too full of emotion, mainly rage. It's like you two are polar opposites. I think I'll stick with the logical son of Helix Rule."

Gideon slowly sits up straight in his chair and reaches for his cup of coffee. "If I'm so logical, how the hell did I get tied up in that nonsense last night? I can't remember the last time I took a swing at someone. No wonder I'm sore today. Even if the son of a bitch didn't hit me, I'd probably be aching all over."

"That's because you spend too much time being civilized and logical here in this hotel. You need to get out and enjoy the world, man. What exactly was that guy's problem with you anyway?"

A slow smile lifts the corners of my cousin's mouth. "I think he was picking up on the vibe his wife or girlfriend was giving off. I'm not sure what she is to him, but last night, she wasn't interested in him enough, I guess. I was having a good time flirting with her. You know, no harm, no foul. Just adults having a little fun. I didn't think he was going to slap her and then drop her to the ground. Fucking dick."

"So you decided that you needed to defend her honor and beat the hell out of her man. Sounds very balanced and logical," I say, teasing him.

"I didn't intend of doing anything of the sort, but Christ, he dropped her like she was a fifty-pound sack of flour right in front of me. I may not enjoy fighting, but I have a reputation to uphold around here. I didn't realize he planned to take out all his jealousy on the two of us."

His explanation makes me laugh. "So much logic there. She was gorgeous, though. She should be thanking you this morning for defending her honor. What happened after you two left the party?"

Gideon's dark eyebrows shoot up into his

forehead. "She didn't leave with me. She disappeared into the night, and I didn't go after her because I get the feeling those two are nothing but trouble. I bet they put on that show in public more often than not because he's a jealous asshole and she likes to push his buttons by flirting with other men. She's probably waking up next to him right now."

"Too bad for you."

Gideon shakes his head at that idea. "No, not too bad for me. I don't get involved with that kind of drama. I've got a business to run here and a reputation to keep up. Neither of those have any space open for a damsel in distress who likes to poke the bear."

"Be careful. You're sounding distinctly unherolike right now."

That gets me another eye roll. "I'm no hero. I don't think there's ever been a Rule anyone could call a hero. I'm a villain like the rest of our family. I just make it look presentable."

My mood improved, I stand to leave. "Presentable villainy by Gideon Rule. Sounds about right. That can be the title of your autobiography. As for me, I prefer the behind-the-scenes villain act I get to play in life. I guess I better get back up to the room and Sienna."

"Still thinking of going with forcing her to see your point of view?"

Throwing my head back in laughter, I say, "I think I'm going to go with charm and see where that gets me."

"Charm?" Gideon asks as he lets his discriminating

gaze drift over me. "That's not usually your style. You might want to get yourself a new suit if you're going to try to be charming."

I turn to walk out as I mumble, "I didn't say I was going to try to be some charming asshole businessman."

He laughs behind me and says, "Try the store in the lobby. Go with black. You don't want to look like a goddamned tourist when you go charming."

Leave it to someone in my family to mention that being charming isn't really my strong suit. I'd still take the Rules over the Rossettis any day of the week. Now I just have to make Sienna see that.

As I walk into our suite, it's strangely silent. "Sienna, I'm back," I call out so she can hear me if she's in the bathroom.

But she doesn't answer.

She's probably still angry with me. Time to turn on that charm Gideon doesn't think I possess.

"I'm sorry about what I said. I forget that not everyone views their family like I do. I think we need to talk about things, though, so I'll be here waiting when you come out."

I sit down on the edge of the bed and exhale a deep breath. Barely nine in the morning and we've already had a fight. Is that usual? I'm not exactly the dating kind. By the time a woman and I could be considered a couple, I'm gone from the scene. My job doesn't exactly encourage long-term relationships.

That's all changed with Sienna, but it doesn't mean

I'm a master of how the hell being a boyfriend works. I hope she understands that.

After five minutes, I begin to get restless. I don't hear the water running in the shower, so she should have come out by now. Maybe this is one of those times real charm would work.

I pad over to the bathroom door and gently rap my knuckles off it. "Sienna, come out so we can talk."

Nothing. She doesn't make a sound. Is she really that angry? I mean, I get the idea of killing her brothers upsets her, but this isn't like her. She's a fighter. If she has something to say to me, she doesn't censor herself.

So why is she giving me the silent treatment now?

"Sienna?" I say, pressing my ear to the bathroom door.

Still nothing.

I'm a patient man, but my patience is wearing thin already this morning. "Sienna, I'm coming in."

I expect her to snap at me like my sisters used to when I'd demand to use the bathroom as a teenager, but she says nothing. Flinging the door open, I march in with a head full of steam ready to tell her this silent bullshit isn't going to work, but she's not in here.

Where the hell is she?

My mind spins with possibilities of where she's gone. Did her brother get to her while I was downstairs with Gideon? I didn't think to mention to her not to open the door for anyone when we came back here last night. Christ! Did they get lucky and find her here alone? Did that bastard take her?

Grabbing my gun, I tear down the stairs to Gideon's office, again storming in as panic overtakes me. My cousin looks up from his work with confusion in his eyes and begins to bust my balls about something, but I'm not listening.

"Sienna's gone! I went back up to the room and she's not there. I swear to God if that brother of hers took her again, I'm going to torture that fucker before I kill him so goddamned slowly he's going to beg to die."

Gideon quickly stands up and hurries past me out to the lobby. His assistant is standing with one of the front desk workers, but he ignores her and pulls Sasha away toward an alcove on the side of the massive room.

"Did you see Sienna Rossetti today?"

Sasha looks past him to where I'm standing a few feet away and nods her head. "Yes, about fifteen minutes ago. She walked out the front doors."

"Was anyone with her?" I ask, my heart racing at the thought of how much damage Matteo could have done in those few precious minutes.

Gideon's assistant shakes her head, making her blond hair move with it. "No. She was alone."

"Tell security I want the entire hotel searched, including the grounds. I want her found. Do you understand me?" Gideon snaps at Sasha.

She nods her understanding, but he's already

moved on and turns to look at me. "If she's here, my men will find her. Where else would she go?"

I think I know where she might be. Her brothers didn't come to her. She's gone to them.

"I hope I'm wrong, but I'm betting she went to see her family."

Gideon looks at me like he doesn't understand. I don't either. "Why? And why without you?"

As I turn to leave, I mumble, "I'm guessing like you she thinks she can use logic to convince her brother not to repeat the mistake he made a few days ago. You people with your logic bullshit baffle me. I just hope I can get there in time before he does something to hurt her."

Not that Matteo Rossetti's options from this point on are any different than they were before Sienna went there. If she and I are going to have any chance at a happily ever after, he can't be long for this world.

And she needs to see that.

CHAPTER TWENTY-ONE

ienna

I THOUGHT I'D BE MORE NERVOUS OR EVEN SCARED to be back at my father's villa, but now that I'm here, all I feel is calm. No, this place has never felt like home, just as none of these people who live here ever felt like family, but now that I'm here again after knowing the truth about my father and my brothers, I feel like a returning conqueror.

That hitman didn't kill me. That asshole you tried to marry me off to didn't get to ruin my life. All your plans for me have failed, and I want everyone with the last name Rossetti to know that.

To know that whatever they think of me, I'm not going to simply be pushed and pulled this way and that to make them happy. I'm the daughter of

Salvatore Rossetti and Sofia Bianchi, and their strength flows through my veins.

The house feels oddly empty compared to when my father and stepmother lived here with my brothers and me. Did Matteo send everyone away when he took over as head of the family? It wouldn't surprise me. He always was a selfish thing.

There aren't any staff here either. I can't imagine he fired all the housekeepers and cooks. So where is everyone?

I creep up the stairs of the old villa that always reminded me of what the Capulets' house looked like in Romeo and Juliet. The pale wood steps creak as I step on each one, something I always hated when I lived here as a teenage girl. No matter how careful I was, someone always heard when I came home late or tried to sneak out in the middle of the night.

Yet no one comes out to see who's making their way up to the second floor this morning. The emptiness of this home feels downright eerie. Is it possible no one is around?

No, that can't be. Even if all my brothers and their girlfriends are gone, there should still be staff in the house.

Not that I'm eager to see any of them. I'm sure they'll sound the alarm as soon as they lay eyes on me. My brothers have likely threatened each of the staff to within an inch of their lives if they don't tell them everything that happens here. They would do it out of loyalty to my father. For Matteo, they'll do it because they're terrified. That's the difference between father and son.

I slowly walk down the hallway toward my father's old office where I assume I'll find my brother. Perhaps the entire house is so quiet because they're all in mourning for Lucius Angeloni. I'm sure my family is quite saddened by his untimely death, especially since he was so willing to pay good money to have me as his bride.

That bastard gets no tears from me.

From a room just a few feet away, I finally hear noises. Maybe all my brothers are there together. Good. They should all hear what I have to say anyway.

For the first time since I stepped foot in this house again, my heart begins to race as I near my father's office. I'm not afraid, though. Even after all Matteo has done to me, I don't fear him. He put a hit out on me, and I lived. He thought he'd force me to marry a man I don't love, and he's dead and I'm still here.

Matteo should fear me. Clearly, fate has better things in store for me than what my dear brother would like to do to me.

I stop just before I reach the room and take a deep breath, holding it in my lungs for a long moment before I let it out. My nervousness leaves with it, and now all I feel is the power I've always had inside me.

Just as my father taught me.

Two steps more and I stop in the doorway to look in at the man seated behind the desk. Matteo looks so wrong there. He's too young, too foolish compared to our father. He looks like Salvatore Rossetti, but the resemblance is only skin deep. His mind is nothing like the man's who fathered him.

"What are you doing here?" he asks angrily, instantly setting the tone for our meeting.

I can work with anger. He has no idea how much of that emotion I have stored up for him and all he's done to me in the past week.

Before I can answer his question, he says, "You were stupid if you came here alone, Sienna."

Stepping into the office, I quickly scan the room around me and see only Matteo. He probably did send all our brothers away, the selfish bastard.

"It seems we're both alone, dear brother."

He scowls at my statement of the obvious and shakes his head. "I know you had something to do with the death of Lucius last night. You're going to have the Rossettis and the Angelonis hunting you down for the rest of your life for that mistake. You should run now."

His threats do nothing to my need to set him straight on who he's dealing with, so I walk toward him and stop right before I reach those chairs my father always kept in front of his desk. They used to bring back memories of when I was a little girl when he was alive. Now they make me feel nothing, just like this member of my family.

"There will be no running, Matteo. You don't want to fuck with me again. You have fair warning.

Anything that happens after this is on your head, not mine. Remember that."

He rolls his eyes and chuckles like my threats are as empty as his. "You're a woman with no power. I'll fuck with you whenever I want. You will never have a moment's peace in this world because I will have you married off to someone who benefits this family. You may not understand or care about your responsibilities, but I do, and as head of this family, I have the right to do as I choose."

His medieval way of thinking still baffles me, but I don't fear being married off anymore. Alaric was right. I do have a family who cares about me. It's just not named Rossetti.

"Whatever power I have, I got from our father. You remember him, Matteo? The man I believed put out a hit on me two years ago. I thought he wanted me dead, but it was you, wasn't it? Your friend Lucius told me that. Just a note, but I don't think he liked you as much as you liked him. I doubt he'd be in mourning if you were the one killed last night."

Surprise fills my brother's eyes at my mention of how I found out who tried to kill me that sunny day two years ago. "That was before I realized your usefulness. Now I see it's far better to marry you off, collect the money, and make myself richer in the process."

I narrow my eyes in anger at his misguided assumption that I'm just going to let him marry me off, like it's the fucking Middle Ages and I have absolutely no choice in the matter. "I'm not getting married to anyone of your choosing, so get that thought out of your pretty little head right now, brother. If you've mismanaged our father's fortune, then you'll have to find a way to make yourself flush again. It won't be through me, though."

He stands from behind the desk and points his finger at me. "You always were too self-important for your own good, Sienna. I told our father not to let you go to school in the States. I told him you'd get ideas in your head about what you should be doing. Clearly, I was right. Complain all you want, but you will do as I say. I'm the head of this family, and as the head, I make the decisions."

I can't stop my laughter, which only enrages him more. "What a ridiculous man you are. As if I didn't think these same ideas right here the entire time I was growing up. What century is it in your world, Matteo? Because it's the twenty-first century in the real world, and as I know I told you before, women have rights here in Italy as much as they do in America."

With a wave of his hand, he dismisses the truth he doesn't want to accept. "You're in a different place now, Sienna. You made a mistake coming here today. I don't know what you thought would happen, but you're not leaving here. So much for your twenty-first century rights and power."

My heart slams into my chest at the possibility that I overplayed my hand by coming here. If I did, then I need to find a way out, but he needed to hear what I had to say.

"You won't keep me here, Matteo."

My gaze darts around the room as I look for anything I can use as a weapon. He doesn't want to kill me. I'm far too valuable as a pawn he can use to get money. I just need to find something that I can use to get away.

He takes a step around his desk so he's mere feet away, and I know I have to come up with a way to defend myself. However stupid this may have been, I'm not going to be his to marry off to whatever asshole friend with money he thinks will best help him.

No fucking way.

Matteo reaches out to grab my arm, and just then, I spy the perfect weapon sitting on the top of the desk. I quickly lean over the chair in front of me and grab the metal scissors. At the first touch of his rough fingers on my wrist, I launch into action, my brain focused on a single thought.

I will not spend the rest of my life looking over my shoulder.

He begins to say something about coming with him, and a second later, I plunge those scissors into his forearm with as much velocity as I can manage. My brother cries out in pain, staring down at the silver handles sticking out of his arm. I don't know how far I jabbed them into his skin, but the sound coming out of his mouth makes me think I did enough damage to stop him.

At least long enough for me to get away.

"You fucking cunt! I swear to God I'm going to kill you for this!" he bellows, and for the first time since I came back to this house, I'm afraid.

His eyes flash pure rage, and his fingers stay clamped down on my wrist, making it impossible to escape. I have to do something or he's going to kill me, just as he swore he would. My mind whirls with a mixture of pure fear and the need to survive. I can't find anything else to hurt him with. There's a pen on the desk, but that won't do the job.

In a flash, my mind fills with a single image of what I need to do to get myself away from him. As he squeezes my arm harder and screams in pain, I reach over and yank the scissors from his arm. Blood sprays up from the wound, and I only have seconds before he lashes out at me.

My fingers clutch those scissors covered in blood so hard my palm hurts, but I have a single focus. I stare at the spot on his body where I have to hit and thrust my hand forward.

The feel of the scissors plunging into his skin radiates through me, but this second time it's different. The flesh on his neck just below his ear is thinner and less muscular than his forearm, and the weapon sinks in far smoother than the first time I stabbed him.

This time is so much bloodier too, and I'm covered in seconds as his jugular explodes out of his neck. Matteo's eyes stare at me in horror, wide open and full of shock at what's happened to him. I watch as he collapses to the floor at my feet, blood spraying everywhere on his way down.

The sight is nothing short of grotesque. The scissors, now blood red instead of silver, stick out of his neck like some horrible foreign addition to his body. His eyes remain fixed in a look of complete terror, as if the last thing he saw before leaving this world was the sight of the devil himself.

I step back in disbelief, shaking my head as my entire body trembles uncontrollably. I killed my brother. I'm a killer, just like him and just like the hitman he ordered to end my life.

In the distance, I hear someone yell, but I can't move. It's like I'm frozen to the spot where I committed this awful deed. Like this is where I must spend the rest of my life in penance for killing my own brother.

"Sienna! Where are you?"

I recognize the voice as Alaric's, but even knowing he's here to help me, I can't move. I'm trapped in this room filled with my guilt while my victim stares up at me in abject horror.

"Sienna!" he calls out, and I turn to see him standing in the doorway, his eyes wide with shock.

"Holy fuck! What happened?" he asks as he rushes in to take me into his arms.

For a split second, I think about telling him not to touch me because of the blood, but I can't seem to say the words, so I collapse into his protective hold. I should be crying as I bury my face in his chest, but the tears don't come.

Alaric tilts my head back so I have to look up at him. In his dark eyes, I see genuine concern that seems misplaced since I'm still alive and my victim lays dead at our feet in a pool of blood.

"Baby, are you okay? Did he hurt you?" he asks in a soft voice.

I shake my head, still unable to find any words. Alaric's hands feel so warm on my face, like he's living and I'm nothing but the cold shell of a person now.

"We need to get out of here. I'll get you out of the country today. I won't let them take you in for this, Sienna. I promise."

And suddenly, with those words, everything I've done comes rushing over me. "I killed him, Alaric. He said he was going to keep me here and marry me off again just like you said he would. He grabbed my arm to stop me from leaving, and I grabbed the first thing I could find. I killed him!"

Tears flow down my cheeks and I begin to hyperventilate, making what Alaric's saying impossible to understand. I'm a killer. I'm going to be wanted here and back in the States and everywhere else in the world. I've made sure I will never have a happy day again.

He hurries me out of there, and on the way downstairs, we pass one of the housekeepers I know from living here. Her expression fills with concern, and I follow her gaze to my shirt covered in blood.

Alaric pushes past her and rushes me out the front door out into the sunlight that I'll never experience again if I'm put away for my crime. Fear flows through me at the very thought of not being able to enjoy a sunny day or waking up next to the man I love again.

I killed my brother because I refused to live looking over my shoulder for the rest of my days, but that's exactly what's going to happen now. How could I have done this?

Alaric talks into his phone as we rush toward the hotel, ordering the person on the other end of the call to have a car ready to take us to the airport. "Don't worry, Sienna," he calmly says in my ear as he drapes his jacket over me to cover the evidence of my crime. "I've got you. You're safe now."

But for how long is the question. How long before the authorities find me here in Italy or back home in the United States and put me away for the murder of my brother?

How long do I get to remain free before I must pay for my crime?

CHAPTER TWENTY-TWO

laric

SHE'S SLEPT FOR THREE DAYS STRAIGHT. TOSSING and turning, Sienna talks in her sleep about never seeing the sun and wanting to see snow just one more time. I don't know what she means since she hasn't spoken about what happened yet. All the way back here on the plane, she sat curled up against me, her eyes closed like she feared opening them again and seeing Matteo there at her feet with those bloody scissors jutting out of his neck. Her body alternated between trembling uncontrollably and resting heavily against me as if she couldn't do anything else but lean on me.

My beautiful assassin did what I planned to do and in much more fantastic fashion. I would have only put a bullet into his brain. Sienna stuck those scissors in so hard they almost came out the other side of his neck.

I gently stroke her hair splayed out around her head like a reddish-brown halo as I think about how scared I was as I ran to the Rossetti villa. I never doubted how strong she can be, but I knew how easily her brother would lock her up until he found another man willing to pay the price to marry her. I was willing to kill him to protect her, but I never dreamed she'd handle it all by herself before I got there.

Sienna's eyes slowly open, and she looks up at me like she isn't sure how I'll react. She doesn't have to worry. I loved her before she killed someone. I love her more now.

"Feeling any better?" I ask with a smile, hoping to show her nothing's changed between us.

"Where are we? The hotel?" she asks, confused after the past few days of sleep.

I shake my head. "No. The island where I live."

The rest of my explanation remains unspoken. Where you live now. I can't risk her being found by the police if she goes back to Connecticut, so when we left Italy, I brought her to my home.

She lets out a heavy sigh and closes her eyes. "I killed someone. How do you live with this?"

I don't know how to answer that question. I just do. I did when I killed the first time defending someone I cared about. I did when I started working for Helix and it became a job and not just something that happened because I didn't want to see someone hurt.

I live with it because it's who I am. A killer.

"Are you hungry? I can get you something to eat," I say, sidestepping her question entirely for the time being.

Sienna shakes her head and looks up at me again. "No. I don't think I could keep anything in my stomach right now."

"Okay. Just let me know when you want something, and I'll get you whatever your heart desires."

She curls up against me like she did the entire flight back here and rests her head in my lap. "I just want to sleep. I don't think about it if I'm asleep."

I want to tell her that she didn't do anything wrong, but I know she won't believe that. I do, though. Matteo Rossetti took her from her home just days before her graduation, robbing her of one of the most important moments of her life, and then kept her tied to a chair in a room for days before handing her over to a man known for his cruelty to women. And for what? Money? Killing him was an act of self-defense. She may not believe that now because the act is so fresh in her mind, but she'll see that someday.

And if she doesn't, then I'll have to make sure she does.

This is why I wanted to be the one to kill him. She's strong but knowing what she did is a weight I didn't want her to bear.

I sit there silently as she falls back to sleep, but it isn't long before she quietly says, "Alaric, I need to know how you deal with this."

Looking up at me, she looks so small and fragile that I want to say the right things to put her mind at ease. I just don't know if I can find the words.

"You didn't do anything wrong, Sienna. Your brother would have hurt you if he got you out of that office. So you defended yourself the only way you could. You have nothing to feel guilty about, baby. Believe me."

Tears fill her dark eyes. "Will I ever feel okay again?"

I nod as I push her hair off her beautiful face. "Yeah. You'll stop beating yourself up and realize he created the situation you had to handle. He took you from your life, and he would have given you to God only knows who if he had the chance. Never forget that."

"I didn't go there to do that. I know it seems like I did, but I didn't. I just wanted to make him understand that I knew he put that hit out on me and I wasn't going to take him pushing me around anymore. I bet you think it was foolish of me considering what he tried to do to me with Lucius."

Leaning down, I press a kiss to her lips and smile. "I think it was foolish because you could have gotten yourself killed. That's all I ever cared about."

"I'm sorry I said those things to you about your family. You were right about everything. That's why I felt like I could finally tell Matteo I wasn't going to put up with his nonsense anymore. I guess I didn't think about what could really happen."

"I'm just glad he didn't hide you away so I couldn't find you. When I was rushing over there from the hotel, that's all I could think about. He'd put you somewhere and I'd never see you again."

"I should have listened to you, Alaric. I'm sorry."

She closes her eyes as I smile down at her. "You don't have to be sorry. I'm just happy you weren't taken from me. I love you, Sienna, and I promise you'll feel better soon. For now, just sleep."

I don't know how long it will take her to accept that what happened was because Matteo set it all in motion, but she's here with me and safe, and that's all that matters.

As Sienna rests in my room, I head over to Helix's office to find out if Gideon told him any details about what happened after she and I left the Amalfi Coast. I suspect her brothers know who killed Matteo by now.

Just before I reach the doorway, I hear a familiar voice that shouldn't be here on the island. Unable to stop myself, I poke my head in and see Helix standing with the last person I expected to see today.

Maddox Rule.

I stand stunned as I watch the two of them talk

like old friends. What the hell is my father doing here? And why is my uncle acting like there hasn't been bad blood between them for decades?

"Alaric, come in. Join us!" Helix says like everything is perfectly normal.

My father turns toward me, and I'm stunned at how different he looks from the last time I saw him. How is it possible he's aged so much in such a short amount of time?

Then a horrible thought occurs to me. My mother isn't here. The only thing that could make my father look so terrible is the loss of my mother.

My brain spins with grief as I step into Helix's office. "What's going on? Why are you here talking like this?"

"I'll leave you two alone," Helix says to my father. "Again, I'm sorry, Maddox."

His words hit me like a sledgehammer to the chest. He's sorry. That can only mean one thing since the only person other than me who's related to this brother that he likes is my mother.

Left alone with my father, I feel like I've been thrown into a room with a stranger. I don't know what to say, and as much as I want to know what happened to my mother, I don't want to ask.

"It's good to see you again, son," my father says in a somber voice. "Your uncle told me you just returned a few days ago after being in Italy."

He's making small talk, and all I want to know is why he's here. "What's going on? This island isn't exactly a place you just end up at. Why did Helix say he was sorry?"

I can't bring myself to speak the next logical sentence to find out what happened to my mother. Regret fills me for how I wouldn't stay at the house to talk to her the last time we saw one another. I should have stayed, even for a little while. I could have made her smile instead of being my usual self. Then at least the last time she saw me wouldn't have been like it was.

Fuck, I should have stayed.

I couldn't, though. That place is nothing but bad memories for me.

My father's expression grows even sadder, and he hangs his head. "No, this isn't somewhere you just end up."

We stand there in silence as I watch the man I've spent the last few years trying to forget attempt to find the words to explain why he's come to this place where he vanquished both my uncle and me. The unhappiness I see in him now brings me no joy, as much as I was so sure it would all those nights I lay in bed cursing him for what he did to me.

Finally, I can't stop myself from asking the single question filling my mind. "Dad, what happened to Mom?"

He lifts his gaze to meet mine and shakes his head. "Nothing. Your mother is back home handling everything, just as she always has."

"Then why are you here, and why do you look like

you're going to break down at any moment?" I ask as relief washes over me at the news that my mother isn't the reason he's come here today.

I watch Maddox Rule take a deep breath in, almost as if he needs to so he can go on, and then let the air out of his lungs in a heavy sigh. I've never seen my father like this. It's unnerving. Even worse, it's wreaking havoc on my emotions.

"Your brother Sebastian died of a gunshot wound to the head at Mercy Hospital in Hartford three nights ago. The funeral is on Tuesday. Your mother and I wanted you to know so you could attend."

The news that my older brother is no longer on this earth makes me take a step back in shock. There was no love lost between Sebastian and me. We hadn't spoken a civil word to one another in years. That he was killed in the very way I do my job isn't lost on me either.

As the first flush of the news subsides for me, I think about how devastated my mother must be. Sebastian was her first child. As she always liked to tell all of us kids, it was him who changed her life with my father. However rocky the start of their life together was, none of that mattered once Sebastian came along.

And now, not even thirty years later, he's gone.

"How is Mom doing?" I ask, genuinely concerned for how she's dealing with the loss.

His eyes full of tears, my father tries to smile, but it never makes it to the corners of his mouth. "Your mother has always had a way of handling the bad things in life. This is no different. She's keeping busy with all the details of the funeral and all that happens afterward. Your aunts Chantel and Ilona are helping, but you know how she is."

I nod, understanding exactly what he means. Willow Rule has an uncanny knack of pushing aside everything to focus on the details so life remains perfect for everyone around her. Whatever misery she's feeling is kept for when there's no one around.

"I'm sorry."

My father attempts another smile, and this one ends up a little better than the last one. "It would mean the world to your mother and me, as I'm sure it would to your brothers and sisters, if you'd attend the funeral. I know you and your brother had your differences, but you can put that aside for this, can't you?"

He has no idea what he's asking. It isn't my differences with Sebastian that I'd have to put aside to rejoin my family. It's how I feel about him that's always kept me away since that day he told me to go find Helix here.

"I can't. As much as I wish I could be there for Mom and everyone else, I can't go back there."

My answer brings out the same look of disappointment in his eyes that I remember so well. It's like no time has passed, and I'm back there at the Rule estate dealing with him on that night he sent me away.

"Your family needs you, Alaric. You've spent your time these past few years living exactly as you chose, but now your family needs you back with them."

The way my father says that, as if merely speaking the words makes all that's happened between us disappear, shouldn't surprise me, but it does. As easily as my mother can push aside all the bad to see the good in life, my father seems to be able to forget all the unhappiness that still exists with us.

"I'm already with my family. Helix and Kerry took me in when I was sent away from my home. They gave me a place to live and something to do with my life."

He shakes his head, almost like he can't believe we're still doing this to one another. "You act as if I told you to come here because I hated you, Alaric. I didn't have a choice. You know that, and yet you still hold it against me."

My emotions finally erupt, and I snap, "You exiled me here just like you did Helix! You sent me away because I was a problem for our family, and now you think I should come back because Sebastian is dead? My being there won't bring your son back. My being there never did any good for anyone."

My father doesn't seem surprised by my outburst. Shaking his head, he says, "I sent you away because you killed that man and there was no way I was going to be able to keep you out of jail. You act as if I did that over something trivial. You didn't have too many speeding tickets, Alaric. They were going to charge you with first degree murder. I needed time to get the police to see things my way. No one exiled you, and what happened with you and Helix isn't the same at all."

"Both of us killed someone, so it seems pretty similar to me."

Dark eyes flash fury at me as my father throws his hands up in utter exasperation. "Jesus Christ! I won't apologize for trying to keep you out of jail for the rest of your life. My brother tells me you did something almost exactly the same for that girl as I did for you, but I'm the bad guy and you're the hero."

Rage fills me as he compares what I did for Sienna and what he did to me. "It's not the same and you know it."

"Yes, it is. She was in trouble, and you got her away so she wouldn't be punished for killing her brother. How is that different than my sending you here, away from the reach of the authorities back in Connecticut, so they wouldn't put you away for life after you killed that man?"

"Don't talk about things you don't understand. Sienna's problem was entirely different than mine. She was defending herself."

"And you were defending that girl. The problem is the police weren't going to see it that way for you, and from what your uncle tells me, the authorities in Italy wouldn't be seeing it that way for her either. I sent you here to protect you, Alaric."

I can't listen to him justify exiling me like he's the hero of our story. Turning away, I stare out the window at the island outside. "You sent me away because I wasn't like Sebastian. Now that he's gone, you want me back in the fold. Well, that can't happen, Dad. My exile will continue, whether you like it or not. Some things you can't change back when it suits you."

My father doesn't respond for so long that I finally turn back to look at him. His frown has deepened so it looks like he might never be happy again. How many times in the past few years have I thought about how good it would feel to see him as miserable as I was that day he told me I had to leave the only home I ever knew?

Yet now that he's here and as unhappy as I wished for him to be, it doesn't feel good seeing him like this.

In a voice quieter than I think I've ever heard come from my father, he hangs his head and says, "Whatever you think my reasons were, they had nothing to do with your brother. I'll tell your mother you send your love."

I watch as he turns and slowly walks out of Helix's office, leaving me standing there in disbelief. After all the fights between the two of us, he finally did what I always wanted him to do.

He gave in.

So why does it feel like I've been exiled again?

CHAPTER TWENTY-THREE

laric

"Mark that down in the book of things I never thought I'd see."

I give Helix a side eye glance as he walks past me and frowns. "I guess nowhere is safe from Maddox Rule."

My uncle sits on the edge of his desk and folds his arms across his chest. "I'm sorry about your brother, Alaric. Whatever bad blood there was between you is water under the bridge now that he's gone."

I shrug, not really feeling anything at all about Sebastian's death. "I kill people for a living. Death is a part of life. It is what it is."

Helix levels a disapproving gaze on me. "Finished with the clichés? That's your brother you're talking about, and as you and I both know, if your father looks that torn up, your mother must be a mess. Her oldest son is dead, Alaric. Have some fucking compassion."

"Since when are you all about family you don't like? Maddox Rule sent you into exile here. It's a nice place and all, but you had to leave your entire life behind when he and your other brothers decided you couldn't live back in Connecticut anymore. I guess enough time has passed that you don't hold a grudge anymore? Well, I don't forget that easily."

He rolls his eyes and walks around me to sit behind his desk. "I didn't leave my entire life anywhere. Kerry was with me, and that's all that mattered. I haven't given a damn about your father or the rest of them up there for years. Then again, none of them died. Sebastian may not have been anyone you gave a damn about once you left that world, but you still care about your mother, don't you?"

Now it's my turn to be irritated. "You seem to be slow walking me toward something. How about you just spit it out so I can be fully pissed off this afternoon?"

"Fine. I've considered you like a son since the day you arrived here, so I'm going to talk to you like a father now. You need to go to the funeral. Whatever the problem is between you and your father isn't going to disappear, and no one expects it to. Christ, I don't even think he expects that. But you need to go for your mother."

Confused by his interest in seeing me go to my brother's funeral, a brother I never liked, I sit down in one of his office chairs and ask, "Is this part of that Willow Rule being the Rule everyone like the most? Because you've rarely mentioned her in all the years I've been here."

Helix shrugs. "I don't mention a lot of people I'm in contact with. In fact, I'd guess I don't mention the vast majority of them. That doesn't change the fact that missing your brother's funeral hurts her and your siblings more than it hurts your father."

"In contact with? What the hell does that mean?"

A smile spreads across his lips as he shakes his head. "You didn't think when you came here that no one from back home was going to want to know you're okay, did you? Maddox and I may not be close, but like most other people in the world, I've never been able to be truly cruel to Willow. She's called every month like clockwork to find out how you are. Mothers are like that, Alaric."

I stare across the desk at him, stunned at this news. All this time my mother's been in touch with Helix to find out if I'm okay?

"Why didn't she just call me?"

"I assume she didn't want to intrude," he casually answers. "I think your mother felt a fair amount of guilt about you having to leave home because of what happened. She's had all her kids there with her but you, so naturally, she'd want to know you're safe here."

Leave it to my mother to call the villain of the family to check up on me. I bet she'd go to Satan himself if she wanted to know one of her kids was safe.

Blowing the air out of my lungs, I try to wrap my head around going back there. "I went to the estate a week ago and I swear it was like nothing had changed. I don't know if I can go back now and be what I should be in the Rule family."

Helix smiles. "Nothing changed then, but everything's changed now. Nobody's saying you need to set yourself up in one of the bedrooms and eat three square meals in the dining room for the rest of your days. You can go back and be there for your mother and your siblings, though."

"What about Sienna? The cops are going to be looking for her wherever she goes. I won't let them take her in for her brother's murder."

"Then I've got good news for you. From what Gideon told me earlier today, her family is claiming a rival crime family killed Matteo Rossetti. Nobody's looking for her at all, it seems."

That makes me laugh out loud. "A rival crime family? Who's believing that? The guy got killed with a pair of goddamned scissors to the jugular. Who the hell thinks any professional is killing someone like that?"

My uncle's grin widens. "See, that's the key. I don't think they're telling anyone he was killed that way. It serves the family's purpose to claim a rival family was behind his death, so I bet the cause of death is a shot to the head."

I chuckle at the insanity of that. "So a cover up because they don't want to admit someone got to him the way Sienna did. Whatever works."

"Gideon also tells me from what he hears, none of her remaining brothers have any interest in having her back there with them. I think she's going to be safe."

I shake my head at how damn lucky she is her family cares more about appearances than vengeance. "I'm just happy to know she's not going to have to look over her shoulder for the rest of her life."

The smile fades from Helix's expression. "Does this mean your time here is up now that you two are together?"

That hadn't crossed my mind before this moment because I assumed Sienna and I would have to live here to remain safe from the authorities. Now that neither of us are wanted by the police anywhere, we could live together wherever we want.

"I don't know. This is home for me."

"Well, if you don't mind me giving you more unsolicited advice today, being with a woman means you have to make choices with her from now on. Sienna might not want to live here like we do. You love the solitude of the island. I don't get the feeling she's as happy being away from everything like you are, though."

He's right. I've been used to being alone for so long that it never occurred to me that Sienna might not be happy here. That can wait for the future, though. For now, she needs to recover from all that happened in Italy.

As I stand to leave so I can check on her, I look around at the place I've considered home for so long. "We'll cross that bridge when we come to it. Right now, we both have to deal with the realities of our families."

SIENNA'S SITTING UP IN BED EATING A MUFFIN WHEN I return to my room. Happy to see her awake and finally eating, I sit down next to her and gently kiss the top of her head.

"Where did you get the muffin?"

With a smile, she holds it out in front of me and asks, "Want a bite? Kerry brought it in, along with a glass of orange juice. I don't know where you guys get your food from here, but I swear it tastes better than anything I've ever had before in my life."

I take a bite of the blueberry muffin and recognize instantly it's homemade by Kerry. "She makes the muffins, and I think she might squeeze the juice too. Other things we get from the nearest big island since it's not like we have any grocery stores here."

"It's so delicious, isn't it?" Sienna asks before taking another bite of the muffin. "It's like the blueberries explode on your tongue when you bite into them."

As much as I'd love to sit here and talk about homemade muffins with her, I can't avoid telling Sienna that I'm going to have to go away for a few days. I hate leaving her now when she needs me, but Helix is right. I have to go to Sebastian's funeral.

"I need to talk to you about something. It's bad timing, but it can't be avoided."

Worry seeps into Sienna's expression, and I get the sense she thinks it's something about us, so I quickly add, "Everything's okay with us. It's nothing to do with you and me, if that's what you're worried about."

She turns to face me, and in one of my white T-shirts that's two sizes too big on her, she looks like a scared little girl. "What's wrong?"

"I had a visitor today. My father. He came to tell me my older brother died."

Tears fill her eyes. "Oh, Alaric. I'm so sorry."

"Thanks. We weren't close. In fact, I wasn't going to even go to the funeral, but Helix reminded me that I wouldn't be going for my father or brother. I'd be going for my mother and the rest of my family. I know it's terrible timing with what you're going through, but I won't be gone long. You'll be okay here with Helix and Kerry, and I'll be back in a few days."

Sienna takes my hands in hers and gives them a tender squeeze. "I want to go with you. Is it that I can't because the police might get me?"

"No, actually I found out your family is claiming your brother's death was a hit from a rival family there, so nobody's looking for you for that. I just didn't want to ask you to go because of what you're dealing with."

A tiny smile brightens her expression. "Actually, Kerry helped me with that when she came in to bring me the muffin and juice. She's very kind, and we talked. She made me see that I shouldn't feel guilty about what happened because I never wanted any of it to begin with. My brother kidnapped me and then tried to marry me off to that bastard Lucius. I didn't ask for that. So when I defended myself, he got what he deserved. I guess I was having a hard time seeing that before she and I talked. So I'm okay, Alaric. I can go with you to the funeral. I want to be there for you like you've been for me."

It suddenly dawns on me that both of us have lost a brother in the past week. We weren't close to either of them, but they were family, nonetheless.

Cradling her face, I look into her beautiful brown eyes and smile at how sweet she is. "I'd like that, but only if you feel up to it because you're going to have to meet my family."

"I've already met some of your family," she says with a smile.

I kiss her and shake my head. "No, I mean the branch of the Rule family I come from. Not Helix and Kerry and Gideon."

"I know. I met your mother and your sister, and I think one time I met your father, if I'm not mistaken."

Unsure what she's talking about, I ask, "You met Willow Rule? My mother? How?"

Sienna turns to reach for her muffin and takes a bite before answering. "I lived in Connecticut for two years, Alaric. It's not like I was a million miles away from most of your family up there. Your mother came to see me once with one of your sisters. Gabrielle, I think? She said Helix asked her to check in on me to see how I was doing. Then another time your other uncle, Nick, came to my apartment to see if I needed anything, and he had a man with him that looked a lot like you and Helix. He didn't mention his name and the man didn't talk to me, but I had the feeling he was sizing me up, like he wanted to make sure I was a good person."

So much for getting beyond the reach of the long arm of the Rule family.

"I had no idea. It wasn't too awkward, was it?"

She beams a smile that makes her more beautiful than usual. "Meeting the family of the man I loved? No. They were very sweet. Your mother brought me a bouquet of wildflowers she said she grew in her garden and a box of cupcakes she and Gabrielle said they made for me. I liked them a lot."

Helix and my mother conspired to make sure the woman I love was taken care of when I wasn't around. I guess that's what family's about sometimes, when they aren't driving you crazy or sending you into exile.

"As long as you're comfortable being around all those people, I'd love it if you'd be there with me. Let me warn you, though. It's going to be a whole prodigal son returning thing."

Wrapping her arms around my neck, Sienna hugs me tightly to her. "It'll be okay. We'll be there together, so no matter what, we'll have each other to lean on."

We're two misfits from our families who found one another, and until this moment, I never realized how fitting that is. Sienna may not have any of the Rossettis to go back to, but she has me and at least some of the Rules as her family now.

Who knows? Maybe someday I'll be able to feel like I'm not a son in exile anymore. Until then, all that matters is I have her back in my life for good now.

"I love you, Sienna."

She leans back and takes my face in her hands. "And I love you, Alaric Rule."

CHAPTER TWENTY-FOUR

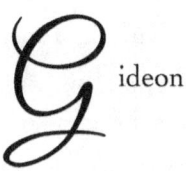ideon

SASHA CLOSES HER BROWN LEATHER APPOINTMENT book and gives me one last look to see if I want to discuss anything more at this weekly meeting of ours. It's nearly midnight, so whatever I have to say to her can wait. I've worked too damn hard all day and need a drink.

"I'm taking that expression on your face to mean you want me to leave?" she asks in that flirty way she always reverts to when she's uncomfortable.

I have to admit after handling everything from irritable guests to vendors who won't give me what I want today that her usual ice queen attitude being absent right now makes me happy. Sasha is efficient to the extreme, but sometimes that means she can be downright bitchy, something I definitely don't need tonight.

"Feel free to pour yourself a drink, if you want," I say as I make my way over to the bar, only halfheartedly meaning the offer.

She smiles and shakes her head so her platinum blond hair twirls around her shoulders. "I've known you long enough, Gideon, that I can tell when you want to be left alone. I have plans tonight anyway, so thank you but I'm going to be leaving now."

We're closer than I've ever been with anyone, including some of my family members, but the thought of asking her about her plans after work seems intrusive, so I simply nod before I take a sip of scotch. I don't pry into her life just as she doesn't pry into mine. That's worked for the past four years, so I don't see any reason to change things tonight.

"See you tomorrow."

She shakes her head again, confusing me for a moment before I remember tomorrow is Sunday. "I'm off until Monday, Gideon. If you need anything, Tamsin will be filling in for me. Just remember that she's nowhere as delightful as I am to work with."

Tamsin is her assistant, and she's every bit as sullen as a person can be nearly every time I have to deal with her. I have no idea why she hired her. Perhaps Sasha didn't want to be the iciest one working at the hotel. Since she doesn't bother me as much as stay silent whenever I speak to her, I pay Tamsin little attention.

Except when she's filling in for my assistant.

"I'll keep that in mind. There's nothing on the schedule that I'll have to involve her in, so things should be fine."

Sasha grins at my subtle admission that I don't enjoy working with Tamsin and gives me a tiny giggle. "For the record, she's a fantastic assistant. She just doesn't like you."

Although I don't care if she likes me or not, I can't help but be curious about what I ever did to the woman to make an enemy out of her. "Really? Why?"

"She says you're cold. I don't see it, honestly, but that's why she doesn't like you."

This isn't the first time I've heard that about myself, and she isn't wrong. I don't fraternize much with any of my staff here at the hotel, although Sasha and I have on occasion spent time together. But it's like the pot calling the kettle black for Tamsin to say I'm cold, especially considering whose assistant she is.

"And she doesn't think you're cold?"

"No. She likes me. Then again, we had that night together, so she knows I'm not as cold as I normally come off."

My mouth drops open that my assistant has just told me something personal about herself. Other than her name, where she lives, and the staff she dislikes, all I know about Sasha is how she does her job for me.

Well, that's not entirely true, but I rarely think

about her sexuality. That she's bisexual and has slept with Tamsin doesn't shock me since I've known since right after she started working for me that she enjoyed both men and women. Sleeping with her assistant sort of surprises me, but if I'm being honest, it shouldn't.

"You look stunned, Gideon. I don't know why you would be after all we've done. She's a beautiful woman. I'd be crazy not to take her up on her offer. Just because you've chosen to remain a monk more often than not in the middle of the beautiful surroundings of the Amalfi Coast doesn't mean everyone here wants to spend their time working twenty-four seven."

I raise my glass to her and chuckle. "All work and no play make for a very happy Gideon. Enjoy your day off, Sasha. Feel free when you and your assistant are having pillow talk to tell her I like being cold. It keeps the crazies out of my life."

She spins on her heel and heads for the door as she calls back to me, "My plans aren't with her, but regarding crazy, security told me that delightful creature you've decided to keep in your rooms is starting to be difficult."

I take a drink of scotch and let it sit in my mouth for a few moments, warming the inside of my cheek before I let it slowly slide down my throat. I've been avoiding the inevitable with Aria, hoping she'd be settled by the time I got back to the penthouse, but if security is telling Sasha there's a problem, it seems my time ignoring the issue is over.

For some reason, I feel the need to clear up my assistant's misunderstanding regarding Aria, so I swallow another mouthful of scotch and say, "There's nothing crazy about what's going on upstairs."

Sasha looks back at me and shrugs. "Okay. It just seems distinctly odd for you to keep a woman prisoner in your penthouse. That's all I meant."

She can be so melodramatic sometimes. Rolling my eyes, I say, "She isn't a prisoner. Think of her as more like an investment."

I get no response to that, which is fine with me. I have little interest in explaining that I paid two hundred thousand euros for Aria. That's between me and the man she used to call her boyfriend, a lovely soul who sold her to save his own skin.

On her way out of my office, Sasha says, "Well, your investment is threatening her security guard. Not that she could actually do much to him, but they thought you should know."

She leaves before I can thank her, no doubt in a hurry to get to her time off. I take another gulp of scotch and a deep breath in before heading upstairs to deal with the problem.

I arrive at my penthouse door to see Raphael standing guard as he's supposed to. Solemn looking with a giant head that fits with his giant body, he stares straight ahead as I approach him.

"Good evening, Raphael. Everything okay in there?" I ask with a smile.

I don't necessarily think Aria lies in wait to attack

me when I walk inside my home, but the thought has occurred to me since she's been threatening a man who towers over her by more than a foot. My prisoner, as Sasha likes to call her, isn't violent.

At least not so far. Then again, it's only been one day since she's been here.

Raphael turns to look at me, breaking his somber appearance with a look of worry. "Your guest seems unhappy, sir. I told her she had to stay inside, and she threatened to jump off the balcony. So I had Luca lock those doors from the outside."

I smile, imagining the two security guards worried what their boss's guest leaping to her death would do to their jobs. "Thank you, Raphael. I appreciate your quick thinking. We wouldn't want her to jump, now would we."

He doesn't respond, returning to his stoic self and staring straight ahead. If Aria has given him that much trouble, he very well might want her to take a leap off my balcony.

As soon as I open the door, she rushes toward me, green eyes full of blazing fury and her long, dark hair flying behind her. I must be out of my mind thinking I should keep this woman.

"I want you to release me! You have no right to keep me here like some prisoner."

That's the second time tonight some woman has termed this my keeping her prisoner. I push past her as she stands at the door with her hands on her hips.

"Nobody is a prisoner here. You're my guest, so

why don't you try acting like it?" I say as I shrug out of my suit jacket and drape it over the back of the black leather couch.

"Let me free. You do nothing with me, and I'm stuck here all day alone with that behemoth you have watching over me," Aria complains.

I close my eyes and hope to God my head doesn't start pounding. Maybe if I have another drink. As I head over to the bar, I look over at her to see a scowl marring that beautiful face of hers.

"Freedom is an illusion. There are just varying gradations of imprisonment for all of us, not only you."

"That sounds terribly interesting, but I want to be free, no matter what definition you go with, Gideon Rule."

I take a drink of scotch and let it slowly roll down my throat before turning to look at her. She really is beautiful, even as she stands there with her arms folded across her chest and pouting because I won't let her leave. Long, brown hair hangs down to just above her breasts. Her oval face with perfect cheekbones is made all the more gorgeous with deep green eyes that stun even when she flashes nothing but hatred at me.

"What's wrong? Is lounging around my penthouse difficult? Is it some kind of chore for you? My chef makes you food people pay dearly for." I look around my home and add, "And on top of that, I'm willing to bet you've never spent a day in a place as luxurious as this."

My questions are met with a scowl, and she

marches over to stand in front of me. Just a few inches shorter than my six foot four height, she levels her gaze on my face with such disgust that I feel like I should turn away.

"You paid all that money for me, but you barely talk to me, much less do anything else. Why don't you just let me go?"

I lift my glass to my lips and take another sip of twelve-year-old scotch. "Because I didn't pay for you."

Aria has no idea what I'm talking about, and at this moment, I have no interest in explaining myself. We stand there facing off, two people staring at one another until the other breaks.

I watch her grow more frustrated by the moment, but she really is stunning. Something about green eyes never fails to intrigue me, and hers are the color of dark emeralds. The longer I stare at her, the more I see flecks of gold dance around her pupils. She looks exotic, like something foreign washed up on the shore that rivals anything beautiful I've seen on the Amalfi Coast.

Finally, she gives in, her entire body trembling when she realizes she can't convince me to let her go. "What do you mean you didn't pay for me? Franco told me you did. I told him he was crazy and that I wasn't going to be sold to anyone, but he told me you bought me, which by the way isn't legal."

"Well, I didn't. I paid for something else entirely."

"Then why won't you set me free? What good do I do you? I've been here for more than a day already, and not once have you said more than ten words to me before now, and that's only because I'm forcing you to."

Her delusions amuse me, so I smile and shake my head. "You couldn't force me to do anything, Aria. As for why I won't let you go, that's my business. For now, you'll stay right here in this hotel in this penthouse where you want for nothing. As for how much I speak to you, that depends. Right now, this conversation is over since I want to go to bed. I've had a long day, and nothing is more desirable to me than sleep at this moment."

When I turn to walk to my bedroom, she touches my forearm, sending a rush of excitement coursing through my body. I can't deny how desirable she is and the effect she has on me. I felt it that night at Angeloni's villa, and as I stand here with her now, I'm already hard.

"Nothing?" she asks, her eyes full of something I can't place at the moment. Seduction? Manipulation? Whatever it is, she knows how to use it because all I can think of as she looks at me is how much I'd like to be balls deep inside her right now.

Aria steps toward me, brushing her fingertips over the front of my black dress shirt. "I will do anything you want. Name it. Just don't make me sit in this penthouse alone for another day."

I let my gaze drift down her body, exciting me even more. Beautiful with curves most men would love, she's nothing short of breathtaking in the pale yellow sundress she's wearing.

Unfortunately for her, I don't need that in my life. Want is an entirely different story, however.

Dragging my fingertip along her collarbone, I smile at the thought of what she's willing to give me. "I'm not the kind of man you should offer anything to. Trust me, I'll take it all."

"Whatever you want as long as you don't make me feel like a prisoner, Gideon."

"I'm not a man who plays games. If I do as you want, I'll expect something in return. Something big."

As I speak, I stare into her eyes to make sure she understands the bargain she's about to make. I'm not the Devil, but I'm closer than she's used to, for sure.

She hesitates for a moment before answering, "I'll do whatever you demand if you let me feel like I'm not trapped here. All I ask is one thing."

Intrigued that she thinks she should be bargaining for even more at this moment, I ask, "And that is?"

"Don't let any harm come to me. If you do that, then I'll do whatever you command me to. I'll be at your beck and call for anything and everything you want. Just keep me safe and let me feel like I'm not a prisoner."

She wants a protector and is willing to trade anything to get one, including her body? That's an offer I can't pass up. I'd be insane to even consider saying no.

I press my hand to hers and shake it to seal the

deal. "Done. You're mine to do as I please whenever and wherever I please, and in return, I promise to keep you safe. Welcome to the Villa Aurelia."

Sliding my arm around her waist, I pull her to me so she can feel how hard she makes me. "Let me show you to your new bedroom, Aria."

Her eyes grow wide, but in them I see not fear but desire. Good. She bartered with her body, and now I plan on using it as payment as often as I want, and I expect her willing compliance.

"Know this," I warn her. "I expect you to obey me. Do that and we'll get along fine."

In a trembling voice, she asks, "And if I don't?"

"I have a reputation for being aloof. You don't want to see how cold I can be. Be a good girl, Aria, and we'll get along fine."

As I escort her to the bedroom, I sense fear begin to grow in her. She thought she escaped a bad man and found a good one in me. But she didn't.

She found a villain.

GIDEON AND ARIA'S STORY CONTINUES IN RUTHLESS TOUCH (BORN VILLAINS #2). GET YOUR COPY TODAY!

ABOUT THE AUTHOR

Abbi Cook grew up wondering if she was different because she always wanted to know more about the villain than the hero in the stories she read. When she got older, she found there were others in the world like her and devoured their writing, loving every dark word. She's written her own tales for years, but in 2019 she decided it was time to take the next step and publish them. She's never looked back since that day.

Readers can find her at her website at abbicook.com, on FB and IG, and through email at abbicookauthor@gmail.com

BOOKS BY ABBI

Captive Heart (FREE standalone prequel to the Captive Hearts series)

Behind The Mask (Captive Hearts #1)

Beneath The Surface (Captive Hearts #2)

Beyond The Lies (Captive Hearts #3)

Captive Hearts: A Dark Romance Mafia Collection

Covet (Sins Duet #1)

Corrupt (Sins Duet #2)

The Sins Duet

Rule (Villains Club #1)

Take (Villains Club #2)

Burn (Villains Club #3)

Play (Villains Club #4)

Bang (Villains Club #5)

Villains Club Collection

Savage Mine (A FREE Born Villains Prequel)

Savage Heart (Born Villains #1)

Ruthless Touch (Born Villains #2)

And be sure to sign up for Abbi's newsletter if you haven't already! You don't want to miss a delicious word and all the great things with each release, and subscribers receive a FREE book just for signing up!

www.ingramcontent.com/pod-product-compliance
Lightning Source LLC
Chambersburg PA
CBHW020313200626
46814CB00006BA/2219